One More Thing

One
More Thing

STORIES AND *other* STORIES

 B.J. Novak

ALFRED A. KNOPF · NEW YORK · 2014

Novak

THIS IS A BORZOI BOOK
PUBLISHED BY ALFRED A. KNOPF

All rights reserved. Published in the United States by Alfred A. Knopf,
a division of Random House LLC, New York, and in Canada by Random House
of Canada Limited, Toronto, Penguin Random House Companies.

www.aaknopf.com

Knopf, Borzoi Books, and the colophon are registered trademarks of
Random House LLC.

Selected stories first appeared in *The New Yorker* (November 2013),
Nautilus (December 2013), *Zoetrope: All-Story* (Winter 2013/2014),
and in *Playboy* (January/February 2014).

Library of Congress Cataloging-in-Publication Data

Novak, B. J., date.
[Short stories. Selections]
One more thing : stories and other stories / B. J. Novak.
pages   cm
ISBN 978-0-385-35183-6 (hardcover) — ISBN 978-0-385-35184-3 (eBook)
I. Title.
PS3614.O9255A6 2014
813'.6—dc23   2013044121

Jacket design by Hum Creative

Manufactured in the United States of America
First Edition

To the Reader

CONTENTS

The Rematch   · 3 ·

Dark Matter   · 8 ·

No One Goes to Heaven to See Dan Fogelberg   · 15 ·

Romance, Chapter One   · 27 ·

Julie and the Warlord   · 28 ·

The Something by John Grisham   · 34 ·

The Girl Who Gave Great Advice   · 41 ·

All You Have to Do   · 43 ·

'Rithmetic   · 45 ·

The Ambulance Driver   · 50 ·

Walking on Eggshells (or: When I Loved
   Tony Robbins)   · 54 ·

The Impatient Billionaire and the Mirror for Earth   · 58 ·

Missed Connection: Grocery spill at 21st and
   6th 2:30 pm on Wednesday   · 62 ·

I Never Want to Walk on the Moon · 65 ·

Sophia · 68 ·

The Comedy Central Roast of Nelson Mandela · 87 ·

They Kept Driving Faster and Outran the Rain · 94 ·

The Man Who Invented the Calendar · 96 ·

The Ghost of Mark Twain · 102 ·

The Beautiful Girl in the Bookstore · 108 ·

MONSTER: The Roller Coaster · 110 ·

Kellogg's (or: The Last Wholesome Fantasy
  of the Middle-School Boy) · 116 ·

The Man Who Posted Pictures of Everything He Ate · 139 ·

Closure · 141 ·

Kindness Among Cakes · 148 ·

Quantum Nonlocality and the Death of Elvis Presley · 149 ·

If I Had a Nickel · 155 ·

A Good Problem to Have · 159 ·

Johnny Depp, Fate, and the Double-Decker
  Hollywood Tour Bus · 168 ·

Being Young Was Her Thing · 170 ·

Angel Echeverria, Comediante Superpopular · 171 ·

The Market Was Down · 174 ·

The Vague Restaurant Critic · 177 ·

One of These Days, We Have to Do
  Something About Willie · 178 ·

Wikipedia Brown and the Case of the Missing Bicycle · 195 ·

Regret Is Just Perfectionism Plus Time · 197 ·

Chris Hansen at the Justin Bieber Concert · 198 ·

Great Writers Steal · 201 ·

Confucius at Home · 203 ·

War · 204 ·

If You Love Something · 205 ·

Just an Idea · 206 ·

Heyyyyy, Rabbits · 209 ·

The Best Thing in the World Awards · 210 ·

Bingo · 217 ·

Marie's Stupid Boyfriend · 219 ·

Pick a Lane · 220 ·

"Everyone Was Singing the Same Song":
  The Duke of Earl Recalls His Trip to
    America in June of 1962 · 222 ·

The Pleasure of Being Right · 225 ·

Strange News · 226 ·

Never Fall in Love · 230 ·

The World's Biggest Rip-Off   · 231 ·

The Walk to School on the Day After Labor Day   · 235 ·

Kate Moss   · 236 ·

Welcome to Camp Fantastic for Gifted Teens   · 237 ·

There Is a Fine Line Between Why and Why Not   · 240 ·

The Man Who Told Us About Inflatable Women   · 241 ·

A New Hitler   · 243 ·

Constructive Criticism   · 244 ·

The Bravest Thing I Ever Did   · 248 ·

Rome   · 249 ·

The Literalist's Love Poem   · 251 ·

J. C. Audetat, Translator of *Don Quixote*   · 252 ·

Discussion Questions   · 272 ·

Acknowledgments   · 275 ·

One More Thing

⌐→ The Rematch

In the aftermath of an athletic humiliation on an unprecedented scale—a loss to a tortoise in a footrace so staggering that, his tormenters teased, it would not only live on in the record books, but would transcend sport itself, and be taught to children around the world in textbooks and bedtime stories for centuries; that hundreds of years from now, children who had never heard of a "tortoise" would learn that it was basically a fancy type of turtle from hearing about this very race—the hare retreated, understandably, into a substantial period of depression and self-doubt.

The hare gained weight, then lost weight; turned to religion, then another less specific religion. The hare got into yoga; shut himself indoors on a self-imposed program to read all the world's great novels; then traveled the world; then did some volunteer work. Everything helped a little bit, at first; but nothing really helped. After a while, the hare realized what the simplest part of him had known from the beginning: he was going to have to rematch the tortoise.

"No," came the word from the tortoise's spokesperson. "The tortoise prefers to focus on the future, not relive the past. The tortoise is focused full-time on inspiring a new generation with the lessons of dedication and persistence through his popular speaking tours and his charitable work with the Slow and Steady Foundation."

The smugness and sanctimony of the tortoise's response infuriated the hare. *"The lessons of dedication and persistence"?* Had everyone forgotten that the hare had taken *six naps* throughout the race (!)—unequivocally guaranteeing victory to anyone—a horse, a dog, a worm, a *leaf,* depending on the wind—*anyone* lucky enough to be matched against the hare at this reckless, perspectiveless, and now-forever-lost peak phase of his career, an offensive period of his own life that he had obsessed about and tried in vain to forgive himself for ever since? How could anyone think the tortoise was relevant to any of this? A minor detail of the race, known to few but obsessives (of which there were still plenty), was that there had been a gnat clinging to the leg of the tortoise throughout the entire contest: was this gnat, too, worthy of being celebrated as a hero, full of counterlogical lessons and nonsensical insight like "Right place, right time takes down talent in its prime"? Or "Hang on to a tortoise's leg, who knows where it will lead"?

No—the lesson of this story has nothing to do with the tortoise, thought the hare, and everything to do with the hare. How he had let himself become so intoxicated with the aspects of his talent that were rare that he had neglected the much more common aspects of his character that also, it so happened, were more important—things like always doing your best, and never taking success for granted, and keeping enough pride burning inside to fuel your success but not so much to burn it down. Now, the hare knew these things. Now. Now that it was too late.

Or was it? What was that lesson again? Slow and steady?

The hare started running again, every day, even though there was no race planned. He ran a mile every morning, then two, then ten.

Before long, he added an afternoon run to his training routine—a slower one, with a different goal in mind. On this run, he made a point to start a conversation with everyone he came across. "Boy, I sure would love to race that tortoise again someday. You think anyone would want to watch it, though?" Then he would shrug it off and jog along to the next stranger. "Hey, what do you think would happen if I raced that tortoise again? Ya think I'd win this time? Or do you think pride would get the better of me all over again?" Then he'd shrug and run off again, at a provocatively medium pace.

Slowly, steadily, anticipation built for a tortoise-hare rematch. After a while it became all that anyone could talk about, and eventually, the questions made their way to the tortoise.

"No," said the tortoise, but this time his "no" just led to more questions. "No" now, or "no" ever? Would he *ever* rematch the hare? If so, when, and under what conditions? If not, why? Could he at least say "maybe"?

No, said the tortoise again; never. They kept asking, and he kept saying no, until eventually, everyone gave up and stopped asking. And that's when the tortoise, sad and dizzy at having all this attention given to him and then taken away, impulsively said, Yes, okay, I bet I can beat this hare again. Yes.

I'm undefeated against the hare, thought the tortoise. *Actually, I'm 1–0—I'm undefeated in my entire racing career! How do you win a race? Slow and steady, that's what they say, right? Well, I invented slow and steady. This is good. This will be good. One time could have been a fluke. Twice, there'll be no question.*

The race was set in ten days' time. The tortoise set out to replicate what seemed to have worked the first time, which was nothing in particular: simple diet, some walking around. A little of this, a little of that. He didn't want to overthink it. He was going to mainly just focus on being slow and steady.

The hare trained like no one had ever trained for anything. He ran fifteen miles every morning and fifteen every afternoon. He watched tapes of his old races. He slept eight hours every night, which is practically unheard of for a hare, and he did it all under a wall taped full of the mean, vicious things everyone had said about him in all the years since the legendary race that had ruined his life.

On the day of the race, the tortoise and hare met for the first time in five years at the starting line, and shared a brief, private conversation as their whole world watched.

"Good luck, hare," said the tortoise, as casual as ever. "Whoa! You know what's funny—do that again—huh, from this angle you look like a duck. Now you look like a hare again. Funny. Anyway, good luck, hare!"

"And good luck to you, tortoise," whispered the hare, leaning in close. "And just so you know—nobody knows this, and if you tell anyone I said it, I'll deny it—but I'm not really a hare. I'm a rabbit."

This wasn't true—the hare just said it to fuck with him.

"On your mark, get set, *GO!*"

There was a loud bang, and the tortoise and hare both took off from the starting line.

Never, in the history of competition—athletic or otherwise, human or otherwise, mythical or otherwise—has anyone ever kicked anyone's ass by the order of magnitude that the hare kicked the ass of that goddamn fucking tortoise that afternoon.

Within seconds, the hare was in the lead by hundreds of yards. Within minutes, the hare had taken the lead by more than a mile. The tortoise crawled on, slow and steady, but as he became anxious at having lost sight of his competitor and panicked over what he seemed to have done to his legacy, he started speeding up: less slow, less steady. But it hardly mattered. Before long—

less than twenty minutes after the seven-mile race had begun—
word worked its way back to the beginning of the race that the
hare had not only won the contest, and had not only recorded a
time that was a personal best, but had also set world records not
only for all hares but also for leporids and indeed for all mam-
mals under twenty pounds. When news reached the tortoise,
still essentially under the banner of the starting line, he fainted.
"Oh, now *he's* napping?! Isn't *that* rich," heckled a nearby goat,
drunk on radish wine.

Those who didn't know the context—who hadn't heard about
the first race—never realized what was so important about this
one. "A tortoise raced a hare, and the hare won? Okay." They
didn't understand the story, so they didn't repeat it, and it never
became known. But those who were there for both contests
knew what was so special about what they had witnessed: slow
and steady wins the race, till truth and talent claim their place.

Dark Matter

"And that's the puzzling thing about dark matter," said the scientist at the end of our planetarium tour. "It makes up over ninety percent of the universe, and yet nobody knows what it is!"

People on the tour chuckled politely, like *Wow, isn't that a fun fact?*

But I looked closer at the scientist, and I could tell something from the smirky little smile on his fat smug face:

This motherfucker knew exactly *what dark matter was.*

"So as you look up at the skies tonight, I hope you have a little more perspective, knowing more about what we know—and *don't* know—about our vast and magical . . ." etcetera etcetera.

Everyone clapped and the tour guide smiled that smug smile I mentioned before and waved goodbye without opening his fingers like the huge fat nerd that he was. Everyone else on the tour headed back to their cars, but I kind of sidled up to the scientist with quite a little fake smile of my own.

Two can play this game, fatso.

"Pretty interesting tour you gave there," I said. "Lotta interesting facts."

"I'm glad you had a good time!" he said with that smug smile again.

"Oh, I did, I did," I lied. "In fact, I'd like to ask you something about Saturn." I gestured to a dark corner of the hallway.

"Sure," he said, still smiling at me and ignoring my pointing. "What would you like to know?"

"Over there, over there," I said to the fat fuck, pointing to the dark corner. "Past by where the coats are. There's a diorama of Saturn that I think is all fucked up. The rings and stuff. Come here. I want your *expert* opinion."

"I can't imagine they would have gotten the rings of Saturn wrong," he said. "Oh, unless maybe you mean the mural at the entrance? The one for tots?"

"Yeah, that," I said.

We walked toward the corner and when we got there I grabbed the string of the tour badge around his neck and twisted it and choked him hard.

"What is dark matter?" I said. "What is it?"

"I don't know," he coughed. "Nobody knows."

I pulled the cord tighter.

"We can measure its effects," he said. *"We only know what it isn't."*

"Well, work backwards, bitch! You know what it *isn't*, so what *is* it?"

I pulled the cord tighter, and with my other hand I started pinching him in cutesy, creepy ways. Nothing that hurt, just things to scare him and make him think, Jesus, who *is* this guy? What else would he do?

"All right," he whispered. *"All right. I know what it is."*

That was more like it. I eased up on the cord a bit.

"If this is a trap, I swear to God, I will come back and *kill* you," I said.

I was just bluffing. I didn't want to kill this guy and go to jail for the rest of my life. I was curious about this one thing, but not *that* curious. Plus, if I killed him I'd never get to know what dark matter was, and it was kind of driving me crazy. Ninety percent of the universe, and we have no idea what it is? How are we supposed to sleep at night? Actually, maybe I *was* that curious!

"Come to my office," he said. "I have a little desk upstairs where I'm working it out for my Ph.D. I haven't told anyone yet because I don't want anyone to steal my work."

I promised I wouldn't steal anything at all, and he walked over to a door with a little dull-gold knob off the main hallway. "Follow me upstairs," he said. I followed him, even though I wouldn't really call it upstairs—it was just a few stairs, like the number they put at the entrance to a library to make it look fancy. Maybe to this guy it felt like a full-size staircase.

At the top of the stairs was a small room with no windows and no decorations or anything, not even a poster of the moon: just a couple of desks with computers, some papers, empty cups and crumpled wrappers. At first I was disappointed. But then I realized that's how you know it's a serious place—just for scientists, and guys like me.

"This one is my coworker's desk," he said, pointing to the one at the other end of the room. "He's not coming in today, though. He's working on cosmic interference. He's on a dead end but doesn't know it yet, ha."

The scientist closed the door behind us. I noticed he didn't look scared anymore. Now he seemed kind of happy, or something. His eyes darted around the room, and he started pacing in little back-and-forth steps, like halfway between pacing and just shifting his weight from foot to foot. It was actually kind of cute. I could imagine being his mom and loving him a lot, if that makes sense.

"Okay," he said. "Okay. We only know what dark matter is from the gravitational field around other objects, right? Okay.

We know that certain galaxies have different weights with regard to the light they emit. And people have tried to measure the light with different . . . Okay. Wait. Let me start another different way. We all know what black holes are, right? Actually, that's not the best . . . Wait. Maybe . . . Okay."

The way he kept starting and stopping made it hard to know when I should pay very close attention and when I should just let him ramble on and rest up my brain for the important parts. And then, right in the middle of a part that did sound important, my phone started buzzing in my pocket.

"One second," I said.

"Go ahead," he said quickly.

"I'll just pick it up to put it on silent," I said. "I won't even look at who it is."

I went to turn the ringer off, but it's basically impossible to pick up your phone when it's buzzing and literally not even look at who it is, and also I knew if I didn't look, it would probably just distract me even more, since I'd be wondering who it was the whole time, and I needed to focus all my concentration on the scientist. So I looked.

Well, wouldn't you know it: all the friends I had asked earlier if they wanted to come to the planetarium with me—oh, *now* they're interested. *"You still going?" "Hey, man, just got up." "Sounds fun, when?"* Lazy fucks! Too late, I've been here for over an hour! I really couldn't believe these guys. Didn't they realize how much interesting shit there was to see and do in this world if you just woke up at a normal fucking time like a normal fucking person?

I put the phone back in my pocket.

"Sorry about that," I said.

"No problem, no problem," said the scientist. "So, okay. Do you know what a quasar is? We know that quasars are a paradox because they emit great amounts of energy despite being close enough to a black hole to be swallowed up by it. Right? Okay. So . . ."

All of a sudden another thought jumped into my mind, and I couldn't tell if I was just being paranoid or what—but it suddenly occurred to me that maybe it was possible that all my friends went to the same party the night before without telling me, and *that's* why they all woke up so late and then all texted me at the same time.

"Uh-huh, wow, whoa, that's crazy," I said, while I thought about whether I should give them the benefit of the doubt and still make plans to meet up with them later, or whether I should hold off on making plans until I could find a way to prove definitively whether or not they had all fucked me over, in which case I would still meet up with them but only to tell them to go fuck themselves. I really hoped it wouldn't come to that, though, because I had gotten pretty excited to see the looks on their faces when I told them about dark matter and about how nobody in the world knew what it was except the scientist and us.

Also, to be honest, it would be bad timing for me to lose all my friends today of all days because it was Sunday, and Sunday nights always made me a little lonely for some reason. It always seemed to be windier on Sunday nights, too—maybe the scientist knew something about why that was. In any case, the point was that on Sundays especially, I really would prefer not to be alone, even though I knew deep down that it was probably better to be alone than to be with fake friends.

"Uh-huh, wow, whoa, that's crazy," I kept saying to the scientist on a loop as I tried to figure out if there was anything at all in the middle—for example, which friends might have convinced the other friends to leave me out and which friends might have just gone along with the peer pressure, and so which ones I might possibly be able to forgive, even if I had to tell the others to go fuck themselves for all time.

Just when I was finally close to a pretty good theory, I noticed that the scientist wasn't saying anything anymore. He was just standing there, staring at me with that same smile from before, only not so smug anymore, like now it was really tender and scared, even though the weird part is that if I had to draw the smile, I would have drawn the exact same smile as the smug one—but I could somehow tell it was different even though it looked the same. And also, I noticed both his eyes had clogged up. "You're the only other person in the world who knows," he said. Then one tear fell down from one eye and then the other. "I can't believe I'm not alone with this anymore."

I didn't have the heart to tell him that nope, he was still alone, so I nodded and walked up to him and shook his hand—a really big handshake, like in a "congratulations" type of way, and when that didn't feel like enough, I gave him a hug right around his fat, nice neck. Then that felt like maybe borderline too much— the handshake and the hug combined—so I gave him one of those solid "and that's *that*" nods and left.

I did end up seeing my so-called friends that night. Get this: they told me they *had* gone to a party without me, but they said they knew it was going to be bad and that I wouldn't have enjoyed it, which is why they didn't invite me. It was a little bit shady, but I was tired of thinking about this so I just decided to let it go. I told them about the planetarium tour and about how no one knows what dark matter is, not even the scientist, which they thought was interesting, and then I did an impression of the scientist giving the tour, which they thought was hysterical. I felt a little bad because in my impression I gave the scientist a lisp, which he didn't have in real life, but that was the part that made my friends laugh the hardest, so, who knows. One of my friends said, "You know, he actually sounds kind of sweet," which made me feel better because that was how I felt about him in my head while I was doing the impression! Even though I was making him sound like a dork, I still thought of him as kind of sweet. And also, he had lied about no one knowing what dark matter is, when he really did know, so he wasn't exactly an angel himself. And I knew he would never find out about my impression, so it wouldn't hurt him. And if he ever does find out about it, through some invention he makes or something, I hope he'll just forgive me, the same way I forgave my friends.

We ordered two pizzas, one of which the place messed up, so we gave the delivery guy hell, and the whole thing ended up being free. My friends are insane, but I love them—you wouldn't believe the stuff they did to this guy to convince him the pizzas should be free, but it was all in good fun, for us at least. Then we watched a movie on TV that was somehow listed in the "classics" category, but it was so bad that it was actually hilarious to make fun of it. It was about a sled.

I was sure I wouldn't be able to sleep that night not knowing what dark matter was, but it turned out I could. I slept better than usual, in fact. I think it's better to not know certain things. It gives the world an extra bit of mystery, which is important to us as human beings.

No One Goes to Heaven to See Dan Fogelberg

Tim, nine years old, leaned next to his grandmother as she lay in her hospital bed. He gently kissed her face around the tubes in her nose.

"I love you, Nana," said Tim. "I promise I'll visit you in heaven."

The next day, Tim's grandmother died.

Sixty-six years after that, Tim died.

The first thing Tim did when he got to heaven was look for his wife.

He was so anxious and excited to find her that he couldn't focus on anything else—not the fact that he had died, not the fact that he was in heaven, and certainly not his grandmother.

"Is Lynn here?" he asked everyone he met. "Yes," they said, but he kept asking. "Is Lynn here?" "Yes," they laughed, "you'll see her in like two seconds!"

And there she was, standing beside a park bench in a spring dress, looking at the same time the way she looked when he had known her last, at the hour of her death just under a year ago, and the way she looked at her very most beautiful, the day he married her, when she was twenty-two and he was twenty-five.

It was a far deeper and sharper moment of first love than the *first* first moment of first love, because now, not only was he falling in love, but he was falling in love with someone he loved; and while the first time, he also believed he'd be with her forever, he was too young to consider what forever meant.

Now here he was, truly, on the first day of forever.

He kissed her for an eternity, which was fine, because heaven had eternities to burn. Then he kissed her for another.

"It wouldn't have been heaven without you."

He took her hand in his, and they strolled out of the park together.

"Oh, and you gotta remind me," said Tim as they walked. "One of these days I have to visit my grandma. Remind me, okay?"

"Of course!" said Lynn. "I would love to meet her."

But first, they looked up their friends, the ones they had shared for the main length of their life together. They brought to each house a bottle of wine that never emptied, and they visited everyone for hours, laughing late into the night, reminiscing and gossiping about who had died and who hadn't. Then they'd wake up early the next morning, make coffee and French toast, and talk about the friends they had visited and whether or not heaven had changed them.

Next they went to see Tim's parents, who were doing very well and were very happy to see both of them.

"Have you visited Nana yet?" asked his parents.

Not yet, said Tim, but soon.

Next, they visited Lynn's mother.

"You know your father's here," Lynn's mother told Lynn.

Lynn was surprised to hear this. "It would be the right thing to visit him."

Tim had never met Lynn's father, but he had heard all about their relationship. Her father abandoned her family when she was thirteen and only saw her once more, when he showed up unannounced at her high school graduation and tried to reconcile, ruining the day for her. She had retaliated by rebuffing him publicly and rudely. She did not want to see him at all, but she could tell it was the right thing to do, and heaven was the kind of place that made you want to do the right thing.

"We'll go together," said Tim. "It'll be fine."

Lynn's father opened the door to his oversized condominium with a huge grin. Of course he would have a condominium in heaven.

"Remember at your high school graduation?" he said. "When you told me to go to hell?"

He smiled like he had been looking forward to saying that line for a long time.

"What a jerk," she said after they left. "Why did they let him in?"

"He must have changed," said Tim.

"And then changed back?"

"Maybe," said Tim. "Who knows how things work here?"

"Well, maybe this is better, because I get to feel mercy, or something. Or close that chapter. Or whatever. I did it. You know?"

"That's a good attitude," said Tim. "And it was the right thing to do. Now you can enjoy heaven with a clear conscience."

The next day, Tim called Nana.

"Hello?"

"Nana?"

"Who's this?"

"Nana! It's Tim!"

"Tim who?"

"Tim Donahue!"

"Eliza's husband? Oh." She sounded unhappy. "Hi."

"No, Tim *Junior.* Eliza's son. Timmy! Your grandson!"

"*Timmy!* Oh, goodness—Timmy, you died? You're just a little boy!"

"No, Nana, I'm all grown up! I'm in my seventies now. Was."

"Oh, thank goodness. I still pictured you as a little boy! How did everything wind up?"

"Well . . . there's a lot to cover, Nana! We want to come visit you. I have a wife now—I want you to meet her!"

"Oh, that's wonderful! Wonderful. It will be so wonderful to see you both!"

"When's good?" said Tim.

"When? Oh. Hm." Nana paused. "I have a bunch of stuff next week. I'm seeing some friends, and there's a couple concerts I want to see . . . How about next weekend? The weekend after this coming weekend, I mean."

"We would love that. How about Sunday, for dinner? Like old times?"

"Huh?"

"Like the Sunday dinners you used to make us, when we were kids."

"Oh. Sure, we could do that. Or we could order in. Lot of options. Let's decide closer to then, okay?"

"Okay, Nana. I love you. I'm so happy I'm going to get to see you!"

"Me, too. I love you, too. See you next Sunday. But not this one—the next one. Bye now."

"Nana sounded odd," Tim said after he hung up. "Or something."

"Maybe she's upset that you didn't get in touch with her before?"

"I don't know," said Tim. "It's hard to tell that stuff over the phone. And also, there's a lot to do here, you know? I hadn't seen you, I hadn't explored heaven—it's not like anyone's going anywhere . . ."

"It'll all be better on Sunday," said Lynn. "When we see her."

"You're right," Tim agreed.

On Sunday, Tim called to confirm.

"Nana! It's Tim. Just confirming we'll see you tonight? I'm bringing my wife, Lynn."

"Who?"

"Lynn, my wife. You're going to love her."

"Who's *this*?"

"Tim, your grandson. Timmy."

"Timmy! Oh, Tim, gosh, tonight? I'm so sorry, tonight won't work. Can we do next weekend?"

"Sure," said Tim. "I guess."

"Let me look here. . . . There's something I have to be at on Saturday. And then I'm actually checking out some shows next week—actually, is two weeks okay? A week from next Friday? Can you pencil that in?"

"Sure," said Tim.

"Perfect. I'll see you next Friday! A week from, I mean."

"Okay, Nana. I love you."

"I love you, too!"

A week from Friday, Tim and Lynn showed up at the door of Nana's house. On the door there was a note:

> *Tim: Tried to call you last minute but no one picked up. So sorry but there's a concert I just had to see with some friends. Won't be back till very late. So sorry. Must reschedule. Talk soon. I love you! Nana*

Tim turned to Lynn.

"Am I crazy to take this a little personally, at this point?"

"This is weird," Lynn agreed.

"A concert? Again?"

"Weren't you two close?"

"I thought so. Maybe you're right—maybe she's mad that I didn't contact her before."

"But then why wouldn't she just say it?"

"I don't know. I guess she would have."

"Well, what should we do tonight?" asked Lynn, trying on a smile and finding it fit perfectly. "We're all dressed up, it's a Friday night in heaven . . ."

"Yeah. We can go out ourselves, can't we?"

"Want to check out one of those concerts?"

"Sure!" said Tim. "Why should Nana have all the fun?"

Tim and Lynn walked through the streets of heaven at sunset. A breeze blew through the pink-and-purple air. Dogs barked, birds sang. Children with old souls finally laughed lightly. Horses, bicycles, and vintage convertible cars shared the wide streets.

As Tim and Lynn got closer to the center of town, they started walking past posters:

TONIGHT! BO DIDDLEY! FREE!

TONIGHT! BING CROSBY! FREE!

TONIGHT! NIKOLAI RIMSKY-KORSAKOV! FREE!

"Look at this!" said Lynn. "No wonder your nana's out at concerts every night."

"Ritchie Valens!"

"The Big Bopper!"

"Curtis Mayfield!"

"Sid Vicious?!"

"Debussy!"

"Is this all really free?" asked Lynn.

"Roy Orbison!" Tim pointed to a sign. "Want to check this one out?"

It was transcendent: a private concert and an arena show at the same time. None of the things that had kept them away from live-music events before had made it into heaven. No sweat or aggression in their row. No songs from the new album that the musician was overly sincere about now but would be embarrassed by in a few years. No confusion or pressure as to whether they should sit or stand or dance or put their hands in the air. The sound was impeccable. So was the stage design. They could eat, drink, smoke, make out. They had front-row seats. There were no crowds. They were literally the only people there.

After a few hits, but still at the height of the show, Tim turned to Lynn with an indulgent idea.

"Wanna just check out the next one?"

"Why not?"

They went to the stadium next door. It was also a private concert in a giant arena. Just as they walked in, John Denver launched into a blasting rendition of "Take Me Home, Country Roads." When he finished, Tim and Lynn gave a standing ovation.

"*Hello, Heaven!*"

"This is amazing," remarked Tim.

"I know! It's almost even too perfect," said Lynn. "Like, in a way, I would like it if there were a few people here, a little energy, you know?"

"That could be the motto for heaven," said Tim. "'Almost too perfect.'"

They snuck out to see the next show.

As they kept walking toward the center of the music and arts district, the streets became more and more crowded. Tim and Lynn started seeing more of all types of people, occasionally even celebrities. For example, Ricardo Montalban. He was an actor they both recognized from the television show *Fantasy Island*, but he wasn't being mobbed at all. He almost looked like he wished he would be, or that at least someone would approach him to ask him a question or to pose for a picture. Tim wondered why no one was going up to talk to him and then, to try to figure it out, asked himself the same question—why wasn't he approaching Ricardo Montalban?

Probably because there were more interesting things in heaven than Ricardo Montalban.

It must be hard being Ricardo Montalban in heaven, thought Tim.

As they got within a half mile of the center of the district, Tim and Lynn finally realized why the concerts had been so empty before.

"Look," whispered Lynn. "Look."

ELVIS PRESLEY! LIVE! FREE!

WOLFGANG AMADEUS MOZART! LIVE! FREE!

L. V. BEETHOVEN! LIVE! FREE!

Tim and Lynn stared in awe as people poured by the millions into stadiums bigger than they could have imagined to see the greatest artists not only of their generation but of their entire generation's consciousness.

Hundreds of thousands of people lined up to see Miles Davis; millions to see Tupac Shakur; billions to see Michael Jackson.

"We can see anyone," remarked Tim to Lynn. "We can see anyone, of all time."

It was almost too much to comprehend. It was a good thing they were already used to love, or they might have fainted from the size of the feeling.

They decided on Frank Sinatra, a favorite of both of theirs, and headed into his concert.

It couldn't have been any more of a thrill. Sinatra was at the top of his game. He opened with "The Best Is Yet to Come," and a crowd of seven hundred million chanted along. Then a song they had never heard before—"a new one," Sinatra warned, making everyone nervous—but it was as good as one of the classics, and they had heard it first. Then "My Way." Then "Fly Me to the Moon." Then "New York, New York." Then "One for My Baby."

"Now, here are a few songs whose artists haven't made their way to heaven yet," intoned Sinatra in the same soothing, ever-knowing voice he'd had in life, made even more poignant here, as he stroked the quaintly unnecessary cord of his microphone. "I hope they won't mind me giving you a little preview, keeping the songs warm for them." And then Tim and Lynn took in the soul-expanding sight of Frank Sinatra covering the hits of Bruce Springsteen, Radiohead, Coldplay, and Beyoncé. Heaven cared not for the limits of era.

After five hours and nineteen encores full of more of his own hits, the concert finally drew to a close. Tim kissed Lynn, and she kissed him back. They felt like they were in heaven. They were, of course; but they felt like it, too.

Still, even after all that, they didn't want the show to end, and when they looked down, they realized what was hanging around their necks: backstage passes, all access, VIP.

"Of course," said Lynn. "Of course we have these."

They went backstage. They showed the badges tentatively to the first person they saw in a uniform, who nodded respectfully and walked them to a wide, clean corridor under the stadium. It was a billion-seat stadium, so the hallway was long, but along the way, not a single person second-guessed their right to be there. Tim and Lynn were escorted along the hallway until they were finally left by themselves outside a single, unmarked door.

Tim and Lynn looked at each other.

"Could it be this easy?" asked Lynn.

"It's heaven," Tim said. "No need to guard the door."

Tim knocked, but heard nothing.

He knocked again, harder, and heard nothing.

He tried the knob of the door and found it was unlocked—of course—and swung open easily. And there, leaning casually against a closet door with his eyes half-closed, was Frank Sinatra. And there, on the floor on her knees, was Nana, blowing Frank Sinatra.

"You got to understand something, Timmy," said Nana, glowing and gorgeous and angry and mysterious as she closed her robe with one hand and the door to Sinatra's dressing room behind her with the other. "And it's lovely to meet you . . . ?"

"Lynn."

"Lynn. Tim, Lynn, I'm so happy for you both. And I love you, Timmy, so much. But you have to understand. When I met you, everybody was dead. My husband; two of my kids; my parents, of course; my sister; all of my friends—not everybody, but, yeah, kind of everybody, you know? And I was part dead from it. I didn't know I was at the time. And believe me—I was so happy and grateful for the love I did have in my life, in the form of you and your little sister, whose name escapes me at the moment. Danielle! That was her name, wasn't it? My, what a beauty." Nana smiled at the memory. "She was my . . . I loved you all equally, all so much. That love was real. And it still is. And Lynn, welcome to the family." She hugged Tim again and kissed Lynn on the cheek. "Oh, isn't it exciting? Everyone's here. There's so much going on!"

Nana took a drag from the live half of a cigarette, which she had neatly hidden between her fingers by the doorknob.

"It's funny, isn't it?" said Nana. "You have infinite time here, and there are infinite things to do, but you still don't end up doing much of it. You do what you love most, over and over."

She took another breath of smoke, which couldn't kill her now. "There's something I think about sometimes, when I'm walking through the town, looking at the different concerts. So many of them were so big in their time, and people loved them, but maybe it's just 'cause that was all they had, you know? There's this guy, Dan Fogelberg. I recognize the name, I think your mom liked him, he did this song and that song. I'm not saying he wasn't great or a big deal or worth seeing. I'm sure he was great. But no one goes to heaven to see Dan Fogelberg. You know what I mean?"

Yes, said Tim.

Yes, said Lynn.

"I love you, Timmy. It's just . . . I only knew you for nine years. And I'm young here. You know? I have other things to do besides dinner-at-Grandma's."

He got it. And he got her, too, more than ever, and maybe for the first time.

"I love you, Nana," said Tim.

"I love you, too," said Nana. "Gotta go."

↬ Romance, Chapter One

"The cute one?"
"No, the other cute one."
"Oh, she's cute too."

Julie and the Warlord

"Okay," she laughed after three complicated cocktails. "Now, you, sir . . ."

"Yes."

"You, sir . . . Now . . . I am . . . Okay. I feel like we've only talked about me. But I don't know anything about you. Other than that you're very, um, charming and, well, very cute, of course. Ha, don't let that go to your head! Shouldn't have said that."

"Thank you."

"But I feel—okay, if this is my—well. Okay: what do you do?"

"What do I do? You mean what is my job?"

"Sorry, I hate that question, too. It's like, is this a date or an interview, right?"

He finished his bite of sauce-soaked broccolini and answered, but she didn't hear him clearly.

"Hmmmmmmmmmmm? All I heard was 'lord.'"

"Yes."

"Ooh! Okay, this is fun. Are you a . . . landlord? Because I do not have the best history getting along with landlords. My first apartment—"

"I'm not a landlord."

"Are you . . . a . . . drug lord?" Julie said, stroke-poking the side of his face with her finger. " 'Cause that could be a problem."

"No."

"You're not . . . *the* Lord, are you? Because I haven't gone to temple since my Bat Mitzvah. Ha, don't tell my grandma!"

He laughed politely. She could tell he was laughing just to be nice—and she liked that more than if he had laughed from finding her funny. A nice guy: now that would be a real change of pace for her.

"Then what kind of lord *are* you, anyways, eh?" she asked with an old-timey "what's the big idea" accent. God, she was a bit tipsy, wasn't she?

"I'm a warlord."

"In-ter-est-ing! Now, I don't know exactly what this is. But I want to learn. So: what exactly . . . is . . . a warlord?" Julie asked, her chin now resting playfully on a V of two upturned palms. "Educate meeeee."

"Okay. Can you picture where the Congo is on a map?"

"Kinda," she exaggerated.

"This is Africa," he said, pointing to an imaginary map in the air between them. "*This* is the Indian Ocean. *This* is the Democratic Republic of the Congo. *This* is just regular Congo."

"What? Hold up—"

"I know—that's just how it is. I didn't name them," the warlord laughed. "Anyway. *This? All this*, here? This is what I control."

"So you're like . . . the governor of it?"

"No. There are areas of the world where it will show up on your map as a certain country. But in reality, no government is in control of that region, in any real way. They cannot collect taxes. They cannot enforce laws. Do you follow?"

Yes, nodded Julie.

"The people that *are* in charge are the warlords. They—*we*—bribe, kidnap, indoctrinate, torture, and . . . what am I forgetting? What's the fifth one? Oh, kill—ha, that's weird that I forgot that one—the population of any region that falls above a certain threshold of natural resources but below a certain threshold of government protection. It's not *exactly* that simple, Julie, but, basically, that determines where I'm based. Once those conditions reach that level, me and my team, we show up and terrorize that area until the entire population is either dead, subdued, or, ideally, one of our soldiers. *Ideally* ideally, dream scenario? A child soldier."

"That does *not* sound legal," said Julie, trying to stall for time so that she could object properly and intelligently, which was going to take a second, because she had had a couple of drinks already and had not anticipated having to debate a hot-button topic like this at the top of her intelligence—especially not with someone who did it for a living.

"No, it isn't legal at all—have you been listening?" Julie blushed and rotated her fork on her napkin in a four-point turn so she would have something to focus on besides her embarrassment. "This is a show of force *outside* the ability of any government to enforce its laws."

He went on and on. The words "rape" and "limbs" came up more than on any other date she could remember.

"What about, like, the international community?" asked Julie, hoping this was a smart question. Usually this was something she was good at on dates, but tonight she was having more trouble. "Don't they ever pressure you to stop? Or," she added, thinking there might be something else there, "or something?"

"Yes," said the warlord. "Sure! For example, there was this thing about me on Twitter a while ago—are you on Twitter?"

She said she was but didn't check it often. "Same here!" he laughed. "I have an account, but I can never figure out if it's a thing I do or not. Anyway. I was 'trending.' You know what that is?" She did. "I'll be honest, it weirded me out. I got into this pattern where I was checking my name every two seconds, and there were like forty-five new mentions of me. All negative!"

"You can't let yourself fall into that," said Julie.

"Exactly. Anyway, it passed," said the warlord. "You know Twitter—before long everyone's on to the next thing."

"What about," asked Julie, downing the last sip of her cocktail as she felt a premature ripple of seriousness returning, "the ethics of it? How do you feel about that? Doesn't that trouble you?"

The warlord gestured to Julie with his fork. "That top you're wearing. Anthropologie?"

"H&M," said Julie, "but thank you."

"Even better," said the warlord. "Do you know the conditions in the factories that made that top that you're wearing? Do you ever think about that?"

"Yeah, okay, no. That's not—nice try. Just because . . . No. And *yes*, I know, this *phone*, right here, that I use every day— but, no. No! You can't . . . It doesn't help anything to equate . . . Look," said Julie. "There's no excuse. But that also does *not* mean—"

"Just in case you're thinking about dessert," whispered the waitress, dropping off two stiff sheets of artisan paper in front of Julie and the warlord.

"Remember when they used to ask first if you wanted to see a dessert menu?" asked the warlord. "Now everyone just ambushes you with a dessert menu without asking. When did that start?"

"I know!" said Julie. "Everyone started doing that at the same time, too! How does stuff like that happen? Everywhere, just"— she snapped—"changing their policy at the exact same time?"

"Get Malcolm Gladwell on that," said the warlord.

"I know, right?"

They both scanned the menus, each pair of eyes starting in the unhelpful middle of the dessert menu for some no-reason, then tipsily circling around and around until most of the important words had been absorbed.

"I have never understood 'flourless chocolate cake,'" stated the warlord, finally. "Is flour such a bad thing? I mean, compared to the other things in chocolate cake?"

"You want to split that?" said Julie.

"Flour is probably the *least* unhealthy thing I can think of in chocolate cake," the warlord continued. "Is that supposed to be the point? That the whole cake is just all eggs and sugar and butter? And anyway, who cares? It's chocolate cake. We know it's not a health food. Use whatever ingredients you want. All it has to do is taste good. We don't need to know how you did it—just make it."

"You want to maybe split that?" said Julie again.

"We will split the flourless chocolate cake," declared the warlord.

"Great!" said the waitress, disappearing again.

"So, do you get to travel a lot?" asked Julie.

"Not as much as I'd like. Now and then we'll reach some cease-fire, after some especially big massacre, and things get quiet for a bit. That's what allowed me to take some time off, travel, meet you, stuff like that. Oh, I meant to say: you look even better in person than in your profile picture."

"Oh . . . Thank you."

"Yeah, I've been meaning to tell you that. Nice surprise. Rare it goes in that direction."

"Ha. Well, thanks. Um, same. Don't let that go to your head."

"Thanks. So . . . Lost my train of thought."

"Cease-fires?"

"Right! So, you know cease-fires—they never stick."

"Yes, I think I saw something about that on Jon Stewart. That must be frustrating."

"It is! Thank you, Julie. That's *exactly* the right word," said the warlord. "It's very frustrating!"

"Flourless chocolate cake," said the waitress.

"Thank you," said Julie and the warlord at the same time.

"Can I get you anything else? Another drink?"

"I really shouldn't," said Julie. "Are you okay to drive, by the way?"

"I have a driver," said the warlord.

Julie ordered a fourth and final cocktail.

Discussion question:

Do you think Julie should fuck the warlord? Why or why not?

⌒→ *The Something* by John Grisham

· John Grisham woke up shortly after sunrise in his large, light-filled house outside Charlottesville, Virginia. He put on a pot of coffee for his beautiful wife, picked up the fresh crisp newspaper from his driveway—he was still a print guy, print had been good to him—and flipped peacefully through the front section as he did every morning until he found something that nearly made him choke on his locally baked bread.

CONGRATULATIONS TO AUTHOR JOHN GRISHAM, declared the full-page ad, which featured a smiling, handsome picture of his face from ten years ago, WHOSE NEW THRILLER *THE SOMETHING* DEBUTED THIS WEEK AT #1 ON THE *NEW YORK TIMES* BESTSELLER LIST. CONGRATULATIONS FROM EVERYONE AT RANDOM HOUSE PUBLISHING. Then, in smaller letters: CHECK OUT *THE SOMETHING* AND OTHER JOHN GRISHAM BESTSELLERS AT RANDOMHOUSE.COM.

Nothing happened for a minute. Birds chirped.

John Grisham picked up the phone.

"Dale. John Grisham. Call me back. Call me back ASAP. Thanks. Looking forward to your call. This is John Grisham."

Then a minute later he texted to the same number: *Call me. 911. JG.*

A minute later his home phone rang.

"Hey, Dale." Dale was John Grisham's new editor. Art was still his editor officially, but he had handed off most day-to-day duties to this new guy Dale seven months ago, and so far, there had been no problems. But so far only goes so far, as the protagonist of his latest book liked to say; so far only goes so far.

"First things first: congratulations!" said Dale. If Dale was at all surprised that John Grisham was calling him and texting *911* to his cell phone at 5:55 a.m., he did a very good job hiding it. "Can we pause to appreciate this for a second? I know this is par for the course for you, but: number one for *The Something* in its debut week? I hope you give yourself a second to really—"

"Where did you send the galleys?" asked John Grisham.

"For you to proofread? Uh, we sent them to your farm in Mississippi on, let me check . . . August fourth. Does that sound right? You always spend July and August on the farm, correct?"

"Not this August. I was here in Virginia."

"Ah. My apologies. Right, the weather, that makes—yeah. Well, we didn't hear back for a couple weeks, and word around here is that you never really weigh in on galleys anyway, right? I mean, that's what everyone told me. So after a couple weeks—we were up against this holiday deadline, and, hey, congratulations again, because obviously there could not be a better time to debut at number one than the Christmas season . . . I'm sorry, John. Obviously, I should have double-checked. I just didn't want to disturb you and, like, hound you, especially being the new guy here, and again, I was told you really never weigh in on galleys. Is there anything you wanted to change? I can definitely see about changing it for the paperback, or—"

"The title of the book is not *The Something*."

There was a long silence.

"What?"

"The title of my book is not *The Something*," said John Grisham.

"I . . . am looking at this manuscript right now, sent in by you to us, dated July second: *The Something by John Grisham.*"

"I just meant 'The . . . Something,'" said John Grisham—careful to calibrate both his emphasis and his anger precisely, not letting either cloud the other. He then repeated what he had just said with every possible intonation, approaching it like the methodical defense attorney he once was, just so it would be entirely, one hundred percent clear to this person named Dale. "'The . . . *Something*.' '*The* . . . Something.' 'The SOME-thing.' Do you get it, Dale?! It was going to be 'The . . . . *SOME-THING*'!!!! I was going to decide that part later!"

"Huh . . . . . Okay . . . . I think . . . Why didn't . . . Okay."

John Grisham could practically see the excessive blank space between Dale's words: more typos, these ones over the phone.

"I gotta tell you, John," said Dale, finally, starting again: "I gotta say, people have actually really responded to *The Something*. It feels . . . deliberately ambiguous. You know? It's elegantly vague. It basically lets people project whatever—"

"The book," said John Grisham, "is about a civil rights attorney who is blackmailed by the El Salvadoran maid he risked his career for in order to sneak her children into the country. Okay? It is not meant to be *elegantly vague*. This is about *right* and *wrong*, about the *limits* of the *law*, about *concrete legal issues* and *specific personal actions*. A good title would have been, oh, I don't know, Dale, off the top of my fucking head? *The Case? The Betrayal? The Immigrant's Trial, The Immigrant, The Threat, The Letter, The Lawyer's Pen, The Blackmail?* Just to name a few?! Or," he said, trying to sneak this one in there, the one he really wanted but was a little shy to bring up, "I thought *So Far Only Goes So Far* wouldn't be the stupidest title in the world, if we wanted to go for something different?"

"What would that refer to?" asked Dale.

"Oh, like *The Something* refers to *anything!*" exploded Grisham. "The point is . . . Look, forget *So Far Only Goes So Far*, it's stupid, it's pretentious, it's not what I do—look. Look. This isn't a *ghost* story, Dale, okay? *The S-o-o-o-o-m-e-t-h-i-i-i-i*—no. *No!* This is about concrete issues of our time maybe more than anything I've written since probably *Pelican*. And thematically, it's about the unforeseeable consequences of the compromises we all make. In any case, *The Something* is, on every level, a *completely inappropriate* title. Okay? Okay, Dale? Do you understand that now? How if you were to get any two words wrong in this book, these are two pretty fucking important ones?"

"Yes," said Dale. "Yes. I do."

John Grisham exhaled, feeling his breath leave his body as he did, like his wife's yoga instructor had taught him to do that one time. He never went back to that yoga instructor, but he still thought about that session sometimes.

"I do want to say one very small thing—not to defend myself, at all, but just to make you feel a little better while we sort all this out," said Dale. "For what it's worth—and the answer may be nothing—people have not mentioned the title once. Really. Not once. Reviews have been good. You know, considering— you're an extremely popular writer, and some reviewers are naturally going to hold that against you, but . . . really, I read all of them. All of them. Everything. I have not read one review that has brought this up."

"Okay. That's good," said John Grisham.

"Not one blog—nothing. For whatever reason—and I know it was a huge mistake on my end—a monumental one that will probably . . . Yeah. Just, for your own peace of mind, you should know that the reaction has been one hundred percent okay so far."

John Grisham said nothing.

"I'll tell everyone to hold off on the next printing immediately until you've had a chance to figure out what you want to do here. It'll be a big deal—first printing is a million, as I'm sure you know—but this is my fault, and literally nothing is more important to this company than you being happy here. Think about what you want to do, okay?"

"Okay. Thank you, Dale."

"And John?"

"Yes?"

"I'm sorry."

John Grisham hung up the phone and looked out the window. *The Something*? Were they fucking kidding him?

And, also: number one. Again. Not bad. Expected, but still. Number one. He hadn't taken a moment to let himself enjoy that. He took another sip of coffee, and as he did, he quietly wished himself a tiny, formal congratulation.

"Congratulation"? "Congratulations"? What was the singular? John Grisham wasn't sure. He didn't need to know. Guys like Dale were paid to know things like that.

Although apparently guys like Dale were paid to do a lot of things they didn't do right.

John Grisham took a sip of coffee as he thought about what to do.

The coffee tasted good. After all these years, he finally knew how to get the proportions right.

John Grisham walked over to his bookshelf. He pictured the hard new spine of a book called *The Something* on his shelf, right next to the other number one bestsellers he had written, like hard, humble trophies, right next to his favorite trophy, an actual trophy, the division championship trophy of the Little League team he had coached back when his kid was a kid, and when people could hardly believe that a successful guy like John Grisham really did coach Little League, let alone was a really good coach, let alone was the coach of the division champions, the Reds.

It looked okay, on the shelf in his mind.

The Partner, The Racketeer, The Runaway Jury, The Something, The Street Lawyer.

Not great—just okay.

But okay.

But only okay.

But still okay.

If he couldn't enjoy a morning like this, wondered John Grisham; if he couldn't appreciate learning about his own number one bestseller in a crisp rolled-up newspaper delivered right to his front door, even now, deep into the internet age; if his book was number one yet again and the reviews were actually perfectly kind . . . If he couldn't shrug this off and move on with his morning and have mercy on a perfectly decent guy like Dale who had made a mistake and felt terrible about it . . . then what was the point? What was it all for?

On the other hand: how did John Grisham become John Grisham? By caring about every single detail. By never letting a single comma go unquestioned. Calling an entire book *The Something*, by accident? What would the man in the photo in the ad from this morning's paper—the handsome, ambitious self of ten years ago, still dressing up for photo shoots, still bringing it after twenty-odd bestsellers—what would he think of that?

Manager, John Grisham suddenly remembered. That's what they were called. Not coach. You coached Little League, but you called yourself a manager, just like in real baseball. Or at least John Grisham did, because he cared about things like that. Or did he just care because the kids cared? *Did* the kids care? And now that he thought about it, his official biography on the dust jacket always referred to him as a Little League coach, not a manager, and he had never thought to correct it.

John Grisham ran his finger along the trophy and thought back to that championship season, and soon found himself thinking back to the day, years later, when he realized with more suddenness than sadness that he had to call Random House to have them take that part out of his bio because his son was in high school and hadn't played Little League for years—even though John Grisham still thought of himself, all that time, as a Little League coach.

Manager.

Little League manager.

It really has been a long time, thought John Grisham.

Now he heard the clock tick. Were some ticks louder than others? How come you sometimes heard a clock tick? Shouldn't it be always, or never? Why sometimes?

John Grisham decided to let this one slide. But just this once.

He thought of his life, and smiled.

Then stopped.

It had been a pretty nice day so far, thought John Grisham; but so far only goes so far.

⌒ The Girl Who Gave Great Advice

"Well," she would say, and then narrow her eyes at the person she was talking to: "what does your *heart* tell you?"

(Sometimes she would use "gut" instead of "heart." She switched those up sometimes.)

"Yes. Yes!" the friend would say, as the girl who gave great advice held her squint and then added a slow, small nod one and a half seconds later. "You're right! Thank you! You give the best advice. I feel so much better. Thank you!"

That's how it happened most of the time. But sometimes, her task was more complicated. These were the times the person would say "my *heart* tells me . . ." (or "my *gut* tells me") but would then say something in a tone of voice that made it sound like the person wasn't necessarily all that happy to be saying what he or she was saying.

The girl who gave great advice knew how to handle these situations, too. She would lower her head thirty degrees and then tilt it back up after two and a half seconds, and ask at a slightly slower pace in a slightly lower voice: "And what does your . . ." and then she would say either "*gut*" or "*heart*," just whichever one she hadn't said before. (This was the part she had to be most careful about. Once, she had said the same word as she had the first time—"heart," twice—and the whole thing fell apart.)

If her first piece of advice hadn't worked, this second piece of advice always made everything all right. "Yes! Yes! Now I know what to do! You give the best advice!" everyone told her. "The best! Ever!"

Even though it seemed like her job was over, the girl who gave great advice knew she couldn't join in the celebration just yet.

First, she had to tilt her head down thirty-seven and a half degrees; and then, after two and a half seconds, she had to look up at the person, nod slightly, raise both eyebrows at the same time, and smile. *Looks like you figured it out, huh?* was the message this conveyed. Even though the problem was already solved by this point, it was this follow-through that would keep them coming back for advice the next time.

After she was done with this part, she really was done, and she could do whatever she wanted to with her face. But she always did the same thing anyway: she smiled, a bright, true smile just for herself, because she really did love being the girl who gave great advice.

⌒⤳ All You Have to Do

I wear a bright red T-shirt every single day.

I've been doing it for years.

That's all you have to do to meet the girl of your dreams.

It sounds easy, doesn't it?

It is. That's exactly my point. Wearing a red T-shirt is the hardest part of it all, and it's as easy as could be.

Once I have the red T-shirt on, I just live my life, exactly the way I want to live it. Maybe I take my dog for a walk in the park. If there's a new bar or restaurant I've heard about, I might go and check that place out, and if there are any friends I want to catch up with, I might grab a bite or a drink there with them. But there's also nothing wrong with going to a restaurant or bar by yourself—in some ways, that's even better.

I wear one with a pocket, but it doesn't matter. Bright red is the thing.

Then when you're done living your life for the day, you just go to this website called Missed Connections and type in *red shirt*. Don't put it in quotes, because some people might say "red T shirt" without a hyphen, and some others might spell it *t-e-e* or some other little variation. There's no one right way to spell "T-shirt." Isn't that interesting? So anyway, just type *red shirt*. It will take a little bit of extra time, but that way you'll be sure not to miss anything.

Then you get to see who liked you. More important: *who liked you for you.* Not you changing your behavior to impress anyone or please anyone. Not you on "date behavior." Just you being you. And anyone will tell you that's the whole point. You want to meet someone who likes the same things you do, and who likes you most when you're most being yourself, so that when you are in a relationship, the person will truly be compatible with the real you.

That's all you have to do.

It really is that simple.

Now: when someone does contact you, and it seems like it might be a match, should you wear another shirt on the date besides the red T-shirt, so it doesn't seem like you only have one shirt? Or should you wear the red T-shirt as always, in case the first date doesn't go well and you want a simple way to check if you caught anyone else's interest while you were out on the date?

That is a very interesting question, and one that I think about a lot. I will let you know what I do when that comes up.

✐ 'Rithmetic

The principal called everyone into the auditorium. Everyone K–8. The teachers and the students. Everyone. Not janitors.

"Everybody, I want you to quiet down and turn off your phones," he said. People weren't much quieter. "Nothing I say leaves this room. And if you tell anyone I said this, I'll deny it." They still weren't totally quiet, but quiet enough for him to start.

"Does anybody *hate school*?" No one raised a hand, and whispered laughter again bubbled to the surface of the room.

The principal made an angry face, the kind of angry face people don't fake. "Oh, bullshit! You all hate school!"

Now they were quiet.

The principal walked up to a whiteboard with three words on it.

"They say school teaches three things," said the principal, pointing with his permanent marker. "Reading, Writing, and 'Rithmetic—short for 'arithmetic.' Which is something, of course, that you know from 'Reading.'" He put his Sharpie at the beginning of the third word. "I think the problem," he said, squeaking a line through it, "is 'Rithmetic.

"What's the difference between this school and a happy retirement community?"

The room was silent again.

"The difference is 'rithmetic! A retired person living by the ocean, just doing a little reading and writing till the end of their days—that's the dream, right? 'What do you do all day?' 'Some reading, a little writing.' Sounds idyllic, right? And yet school *sucks*. Everybody hates it. What's the difference? 'Rithmetic! It's time somebody put their finger on this fucking obvious thing. And I'm the principal, so I'm that person, and I'm going to abolish it. Now," he said, looking for a glass of water to sip from and finding none, "now, are you going to be unprepared for some aspects of life? Probably. Yes. But you know what? You will have phones with calculators on them. You will have friends who can do math. My mom, God bless her—I love my mom, and she still doesn't know whether a third of a cup of flour is bigger than a fourth of a cup. You know what she does? Is anybody here honestly wondering, Oh my God, how the hell does anything get baked?! Of course not, and you're right not to worry. She asks my dad—he knows. Or these days, you ask Google or whatever you use nowadays; you find out in two seconds. And also, it's the kind of thing you just pick up. Let's say you're working at a restaurant, and they offer you a ten percent raise. You'll figure out what that means. You will! It's just too interesting, it's too relevant, it's about you and money. You're not going to let yourself get screwed.

"Now, do I wish you all knew math? Were *great* at math? Were fucking *mathematicians*? Of course! It'd be better. But not *much* better, listen to me. Not so much better that it's worth turning eight years of potential heaven—wait, nine? K-one-two-three-four-five-six-seven-eight, yeah, nine"—he wasn't, as was becoming clear, much of a math guy—"nine years of *heaven* of just reading great books and jotting down your thoughts about them—it's just not worth turning nine years of heaven into nine years of hell. You'll get to high school, and you'll be behind in math, fine. But probably not that far—the other schools in this town are shit, let's be honest."

Here there was a sound wave of school spirit: "*Whooo!*"

"So you all get to high school, and, yes, you're behind in math. But you're so *happy*. Listen to me. This is so big-picture important. You're *so* good at reading and writing. Okay? You write the most amazing college essay, you ace all your English and history and social studies classes—it'll all even out. At *least* even out. Plus," he said, "*plus*, you had the best eight years of your *life*! Childhood! Years you'll always remember—hell, maybe you'll even write a book about them—a beautiful one! So I'm just going to do this. I'm the principal. We are, now, a zero-mathematics school. See, you get what that means: zero, none. How did you know what 'zero' meant, just now? From your incredible math educations at Clark Street? No. *Life*. Context clues. See? So: who is ready to make school something that is only about reading and writing—reading fiction and the great true stories of history, and then writing about what's cool and interesting about them? And also music and art and gym and all that stuff, and math teachers, don't worry, you'll keep your jobs, we'll just put you on other stuff. But mostly, reading and writing. How about it? How about we go for this plan and have the happiest, and most literate, kids in the state—*come what may!*"

The students and many teachers cheered.

"Now I need to know you're all in on this," said the principal, lowering his tone. "Because you are giving up your math educations. That could be a serious thing. I don't want you guys running up to me, crying, 'Mr. McLaughlin, Principal McLaughlin, we didn't learn maaaaath, now we can't get into colllllllege.' You just won't know math. Are you really fine with that? Is anyone not okay with that?"

One small hand went up. A few bigger hands clapped for the small hand.

"Arush? You want to learn math?"

The boy's head nodded.

"What if we set you up with a private tutor? Would that be okay?"

The boy nodded again and the hand went back down.

"Does anyone else want private math tutoring after school and on weekends? No one wants that, right? I really think you'll all be fine," said the principal quickly. "I promise. I really do believe in this plan. I just needed to say that, full disclosure, etcetera. But it looks like you guys are on board, right? I think this is a good decision, I really do. An exciting one! So from this moment onward: I declare, no more math! This is a math-free school! Do you want that, Clark Street K–8? Do you want to say NO . . . MORE . . . MATH . . . EVER?!"

The auditorium shook with cheers. All the children got swept away in it, even the ones who had secretly liked math, their shy enthusiasms for the shapes of numbers and the comfort of order suddenly crushed to death forever by this unprecedented force of peer and authority pressure teaming up on them together, in a surprise attack, right in the middle of their auditorium, where nothing interesting had ever happened before.

"All right. Now, nobody can say anything," said the principal. "Okay?"

The students nodded. Some waved a finger across their lips vertically to indicate *shhhh*, some waved a finger horizontally to indicate *lips are sealed*, and the rest of the students, most of them, waved their fingers in front of their faces in a vague, circular pattern that was their best attempt to copy what they could make out of the gestures around them.

"Nobody says *anything*."

They nodded again.

Everybody said everything.

Soon the principal was fired.

The principal didn't care. He was sick of it, sick of all of it. He figured something like this would probably happen. But he might as well go out this way, right? That's what he figured. He had been at this job for a long time, and he was done. Whether the years had finally cracked his spirit, or had finally cracked the shell around his spirit—who was to say, and, really, who cared.

He retired to a house by the beach in Florida and spent the rest of his days reading and writing.

⌒⤳ The Ambulance Driver

An extra minute could make the difference between life and death.

He always arrived at the hospital minutes before any other driver.

"Hey! Just so you know! It's true what they say! You really are! The best! Ambulance driver! We've ever seen!" nurses would breathe at him as they swept his patients into the hospital and off to their surgeries.

"Thank you," he always remembered to say. "Means a lot. Really, thank you."

The ambulance driver knew he was the best ambulance driver. And he knew it was a great thing to be.

That wasn't it.

One day the ambulance driver told his friend Dan, another ambulance driver, that he had a friend who wanted to be a singer.

"What should my friend do?" asked the ambulance driver.

"Is your friend good?" asked Dan.

"He'll never know till he tries, right?" said the ambulance driver. "Or she?"

"That's right," said Dan.

"So? Should he or she go all out and quit and go for his dream?"

"I guess the only way your friend can find out is to go for it," said Dan.

"Well, as you probably figured out, *I'm* the friend," said the ambulance driver with the bright, wide grin that the truly happy share with the truly stupid. "I'm the friend! I want to be a singer. But not just a singer, Dan. A singer-songwriter."

Dan's face went as white as one of their passengers'.

"Hey," said Dan. "Hey, let's think about this."

"I'll never know till I try, right? You said that. When we were talking about my 'friend'?"

"Look—okay—you want honesty?" said Dan. "People generally don't make it. I mean, I'm sorry, but that's just how it goes! And even—let's say you did. What you do now is so, so important! You're an ambulance driver, and you're the best at it! In all of Grant County, and probably beyond. There are statistics—it's not even close. I mean, come on! The most important thing in the world, and you're the best at it! How does that feel?"

"That's the thing, Dan. I know how it *should* feel—"

"*Hey.* This isn't a joke," said Dan with an intensity that surprised the ambulance driver. "The universe tells you what it wants from you. You just need to listen. And the universe is telling you to *drive that ambulance.*"

"Interesting, I'll think about that," said the ambulance driver. Since when did Dan speak for the universe?

The next day the ambulance driver asked a different person what he should do. This woman was a friend who had gone to his high school and wasn't an ambulance driver—he didn't even know what she did, in fact—but for some reason she always gave the best advice. They met at a coffee shop.

"What does your heart tell you?" she asked as she sipped her hot chocolate.

He said he didn't know: on one level, his heart believed that he should help as many people as possible, which was exactly what he was doing now. But another part of his heart really wanted to see where this music thing might go if he put everything he had into it. Couldn't your heart tell you more than one thing? If you were truly confused about something, which he was right now, wouldn't that mean your heart was, too?

The ambulance driver's friend lowered her head thirty degrees and then tilted it back up after two and a half seconds.

"What does your *gut* tell you?" she asked.

"You give the best advice," said the ambulance driver.

The ambulance driver quit his job the next day. Later that night, he was officially an amateur musician, singing to eleven people at a bar fifty miles away.

His first song, "My Song for You," got a lot of applause, though his second song got none, but that was probably because he didn't know there was a one-song limit. "So sorry," he said after that was explained to him.

But as he apologized to the bar manager, something happened. A voice he had never heard before rose up from somewhere around the center of his body, skipped his mouth altogether on the way to his head, and then, once it was there, rattled around and echoed so loudly that it almost literally knocked him off his feet. "I'm not sorry at all!" shouted this voice, a voice that actually took him more than a moment to recognize as his own.

It was the voice he always sang with from then on.

———

The ambulance driver put out dozens of albums with hundreds of songs over the years, but none was as popular as the children's song he wrote to amuse his young son at bedtime, "I Was Walking Along," which he volunteered to perform at his son's kindergarten class and which was such a hit that he was invited back to perform it there every subsequent spring.

The song went like this:

> *I was walking along (I was walking along)*
> *I was singing a song (I was singing a song)*
> *Got a hole in my shoe (Got a hole in my shoe)*
> *Stepped in a puddle too (Stepped in a puddle too)*
> *Had to roll up my sock (Had to roll up my sock)*
> *Rolled it up to my knee (Rolled it up to my knee)*
> *Rolled it up to my waist*
> *Rolled it up to my head*
> *And then I went to bed!*

Then the children screamed like this:

> *"Again!"*
> *"Again!"*
> *"Again!"*

Do you know what it's like to sing a song that started inside you to a room full of laughing, dancing children, who keep singing it even after you stop?

It feels like the world is made of music, and you are the world.

One or two more people died each year in Grant County than before, but it was always a number within the statistical margin of error.

Walking on Eggshells (or: When I Loved Tony Robbins)

I had seen his picture enough and read about him enough to know that I loved Tony Robbins, or so I thought at the time.

When he came to our town, I found out where he was staying, and I knew people who worked at the hotel, and I knew he was a man who appreciated bold gestures, so I went for it. I entered the room while he was in the shower, wearing what I thought of as my best first-impressions dress, and when he came out and saw me, he immediately asked me what I was doing there.

"I'm here because I love you," I said.

"Your feet," he said. "What are you doing? What is that?"

"I'm walking on eggshells," I said. "To impress you. Isn't that your thing?"

"No, my thing is hot coals," he said. "Walking on hot coals."

"Oh," I said, embarrassed to have gotten wrong something that was so fundamental about him—even though that's often how it goes, I've realized since, that we overlook the few things we're sure we already know. "Oh. I don't think I could ever do that."

"*Yes. YES YOU CAN,*" he said, with the superhuman intensity that made me pursue him in the first place. God, he was like ten human beings compressed into one. "You can do anything you put your mind to," said Tony Robbins. "*Anything.* You hear me? Anything. Anything. Anything."

"I want to fuck Tony Robbins," I said. "That's what I want to do. I want to fuck Tony Robbins and look in his eyes and see that he's in love with me, too."

He looked at me for a while. His face looked very confused and humble, but I could tell by the way his eyes squinted especially hard at certain parts of my dress that he was also, secretly, checking me out.

"No," he said.

"What do you mean 'no'?"

"It's just not going to happen," said Tony Robbins.

"Yes it is," I said, summoning and then faking more intensity than had ever been inside me before. "Yes, it is going to happen. Yes: I am going to fuck Tony Robbins!"

"You are? *You are?*" Something about my intensity awakened something in him. The challenge fired him up in a way that my looks, so far, hadn't.

"Okay. But we gotta get serious," he said, staring at me with those eyes again. "We're gonna get you in the gym six days a week, three hours a day, on a cross-training regimen. It's going to be brutal—are you up to it?" Yes! I said. "We're going to get you hair extensions and super-low-rise jeans and a little yellow tattoo of a lightning bolt on your hip, okay? Because that's what turns me on. Are you ready to do that?" Yes! I said. "We're going to get you . . ." reading this book, attending that seminar, learning these interesting topics to talk about. Yes, I said, yes!

"Then it gets more difficult," Tony Robbins said, and I could tell by the look in those steel-blue eyes that this next part was going to be hard for him, too. "You're going to have to drive by my wife's house, our house, while I'm on the road, and you're going to have to leave things for me—gifts, cards . . . things that don't make her feel her safety is threatened, but that definitely make her wonder if I'm having an affair. You're going to sow the seeds of doubt so that the bedrock of trust that sustains my marriage will collapse. Are you ready to do that?" Yes! I said.

I dedicated myself to the program like I've never dedicated myself to anything in my life. Once a week, on Fridays, I would check in with Tony so that he could monitor my progress. He would stare me up and down, sizing me up, determining if I was getting hot enough to interest him on a physical level; then we would talk casually for a lot longer, to see if I was becoming the kind of person Tony Robbins could fall in love with.

"Don't forget to surprise me sometimes," he said in week two. "Learn all these things, do all these things; but it's also important in a romantic relationship for both people to feel they are learning and growing from the other person." This was especially good advice, and I added *capoeira*, guitar, and Italian films of the 1940s to my areas of expertise. He asked a lot of questions about them, more than you would ask just to be polite.

Around the fifth or sixth week, I noticed something had changed about the way he looked at me. Tony Robbins, the motivator, the man I had fallen in love with, wasn't the only person looking at me anymore; now there was another man starting to come out from behind those eyes that had always reminded me of locked steel gates. And it was exciting and scary, if those are even different things, to realize that I was on the verge of something so big with this new person I didn't know, someone I might never know, something with no end date, no target, no limit.

In week seven, I called it off.

He was very surprised. "You're so close! Let's just finish the program! Come on! You can do it!"

"I know I can," I said. "But I don't know if I want to do it anymore."

"You need to want it," he said.

"You need to want it," I agreed.

I told him I stopped because I realized I was turning love into an accomplishment, and he was turning accomplishment into love, and neither of those things would ever quite be the other. When I told him that, he seemed to both light up and flare out at the same time—like he knew this was the truth, but that it was also hard for him to let go of someone who would say something like that.

But the truth was actually much simpler than that, more visceral. I just realized that I was never going to get over the feeling I had the first time I met him, like I was walking on eggshells.

☙ The Impatient Billionaire and the Mirror for Earth

"If only the earth could hold up a mirror to itself . . ."

Say no more, thought the impatient billionaire in the audience at the TED conference, who found the speaker's voice as whiny and irritating as his ideas were inspiring and consciousness-shifting. He already knew the part of the speech that was going to stay with him: a mirror up to Earth—amazing, unbelievable. Tricky but doable. He got it. Let's make it.

"I want you to build a mirror for Earth," he said to his engineers, who were used to things like this.

"How big do you want the mirror to be?"

"Full length."

"How big do you want Earth to look?"

"Full size."

"Can't be full size," said the head engineer.

"Yes it can be," said the impatient billionaire. "And by the end of today, my head engineer is going to be somebody who tells me *how* it's going to happen, not why it can't."

"If it's full size," said the head engineer, "you'll only see the reflection of what is in your field of vision up to your horizon point. That's not what you want, is it? You're picturing seeing, like, China, right?"

"Yes," said the impatient billionaire. "Exactly. Things like China."

"So let's figure out how big," said the engineer.

"I want you to be able to look up with binoculars and literally wave at yourself," said the impatient billionaire. "But you could also look at the White House, or your grandmother in Florida, or see two people on a date in Brazil. My God, do you realize what this is going to mean for humanity?"

"You're only going to be able to see one hemisphere at a time," said the head engineer. "That means you won't be able to see China and Brazil at the same time. Which one is more important to you?"

"I don't know. Same. Brazil," said the impatient billionaire.

The engineer took some notes with a little pencil.

"Wait!" said the impatient billionaire. "Is this mirror going to burn up the whole planet? Don't just 'yes' me on everything, really think about it: a mirror that big, reflecting the sun, facing us? I do not want to burn up the planet. I do not want to be 'that guy.'"

"No, that should be okay," said the head engineer. "We should be able to come up with a material that reflects plenty of light but not a meaningful amount of heat. Let me talk with the team."

The engineers talked numbers and said they could probably have something up in eighteen months.

"Why not six?" asked the impatient billionaire, trying to force into his eyes the rogue, intoxicating glimmer that he knew had served him well in life so far.

Eighteen, said the engineering team.

Fine, said the impatient billionaire. If you can really guarantee eighteen months, fine.

We can, said the engineering team.

Thirty-five months and two weeks later—more than a year late and seven hundred million dollars over budget—the Mirror for Earth finally went up into the sky.

But nobody remembers how long anything takes; they only remember how good it was in the end.

And in the end, the mirror was magnificent.

After a very short amount of time, the Mirror for Earth became one of those things that people couldn't ever imagine not existing.

When people caught sight of themselves in the mirror—individually and as a species—they thought twice about how they looked doing whatever they were doing. Crime disappeared. Wars evaporated. Meanness declined dramatically.

The mirror changed everything, forever, for the better.

Besides all that, the thing was, quite simply, beautiful.

One summer night a few years later, the impatient billionaire couldn't sleep. The air-conditioning in his master bedroom was broken, and even an impatient billionaire didn't have a way to get an air conditioner fixed in the middle of the night without waking up a wife who was asleep in the same room.

The impatient billionaire's mind started running through all of the projects he had in the works, none of which was going as fast as it should be—you'd think the man who put up the Mirror for Earth would attract the best and brightest and most resourceful people, but apparently not, he thought to himself.

Impatient for nothing in particular, the impatient billionaire wandered outside to his bedroom balcony and picked up a pair of binoculars that had been a gift from the head engineer, but that he had never actually used.

After a couple of minutes spent searching and focusing, he found what he thought to be himself up in the sky and made some specific gestures with his arms to confirm that he really was staring at himself, and not at one of his neighbors who might just happen to have a similar pair of pajamas and late-night impulse.

Yes, that was him.

That was him, waving widely. That was him, the little figure in red, jutting out into the endless black.

And then, after the impatient billionaire had established that it was definitely, certainly him up there in the sky, he made a few more funny gestures anyway, just for fun.

What a cool thing he had made.

Missed Connection: Grocery spill at 21st and 6th 2:30 pm on Wednesday

I was outside the Trader Joe's at 21st and 6th at around 2:30 pm last Wednesday. I was wearing oversized sunglasses and a small straw fedora hat, light blue jeans, a black t-shirt-like top, and had freshly washed shoulder-length dirty blond hair with bangs. I'm 29 but people sometimes guess I'm anywhere from 28 to 30. I was carrying two paper grocery bags. You were walking by me in the opposite direction, carrying groceries, too, but only one bag. You asked if you could help and when I tried to explain that then your hands would be just as full as mine, I dropped a bottle of salsa, red, medium spicy Trader Joe's brand (or Trader Jose's, as you corrected me) but it didn't shatter which we both found interesting. I told you my name was Lila (L-I-L-A) and you told me you had a cousin who pronounced it the same way but spelled it differently (L-E-I-L-A). It turned out we were both from the same area code in New Jersey (551) and we talked about our hometowns for a bit and that diner where everyone used to go after games in high school. Then you walked me home carrying one of my two bags even though I said it made no sense to, and you insisted on bringing them all the way inside for me, and then I made a pot of coffee even though I was only making one cup for you, and then you explained about French presses and Kerrig (sp?) machines. Then we both looked at the clock at the same time and realized we had somehow been talking about coffee for over an hour! You looked in my eyes and said it felt like we had somehow known each other for a long time and I said "I agree" and then we made out on my green quilted couch with a blue stain on the left armrest, and after our very first kiss you pulled away from me and caught your breath and just said the word "electric." Then you kissed me again and we made out until we both looked at the clock at the same time *again* and realized we had been making out for three hours. Then we watched Iron Chef together and then Planet Earth, the African plains episode, and we both agreed how that was totally the jackpot Planet Earth, because so many are about jellyfish or algae but all anyone wants to really see are giraffes & monkeys & elephants, etc. I said I didn't want you to leave and you said "me neither" and you slept over at my place in borrowed navy blue pajamas w/ yellow stripes and a hole in the left knee from when my brother visited me and we both said we weren't cuddlers but we cuddled anyway for almost an hour, and then finally you slept on the left side of the bed which was perfect b/c I sleep on the right. I slept on my back which you said was pretentious and I said "what do you mean? That's just how I sleep! How can it be pretentious?" and you said "like you think you're a beautiful angel or something" and I said "maybe you're just really into me" and we kissed again. Then you turned to sleep on your stomach w/ your head facing left and I said "doesn't that hurt your neck?" and you said for some reason usually not, but sometimes yes, and that your fantasy when you were a kid was to get a bed with a hollowed out hole straight down from the pillow so you could sleep with your head face down and straight and I said, "Like a massage chair?" and it turned out you had never had a massage, so I said let's go this weekend so you could check out if that was similar to what you had been thinking of as a kid, and if it's how you want to sleep, it'd be weird, but hey, it's your life, and you laughed and said "deal" twice. "Deal. Deal." Like that. Then you realized your phone (a Motorola) had died and I didn't have the right charger, and you said that's probably a sign that you should get going anyway and take care of some stuff at home, and I said cool, and then we made a plan that you'd come over on Friday and I'd have to cook a dinner that included every single ingredient that I had in those Trader Joe's bags, Iron Chef style. But then the next day, you didn't come over or call to explain why, or reschedule it. I know that I gave you my number but now I realize that sometimes I write numbers in a scribble, especially when I'm excited, which I was, so maybe you haven't been able to decode it or left a message for the wrong number. I know this sounds crazy to say after one encounter but I kind of fell for you pretty hard & it has been forever since I've connected to anyone like this & my heart is kind of broken in a million pieces. Hit me up if you think anything in this description matches *anything* you remember, and if so, maybe we can chill sometime? You were wearing a red t-shirt with a pocket.

✐ I Never Want to Walk on the Moon

I never want to walk on the moon.

Just because so few people have ever done it, people assume it's this great thing they should be jealous of and should want to do, too.

But is it that great?

Let's break it down. Here is what actually happens.

You go into a space capsule. Very cramped. It takes three or four days just to get there. *Days.* Then, you're still in the capsule for *six hours* waiting to get out. Can you imagine? Taking a flight that lasts three to four *days*—and then, when you finally get there, somebody tells you, *Sorry, we have to wait another six hours to deplane?* Those six hours probably feel even longer than the rest of the flight.

You also have to wear this unbelievably heavy suit and helmet the whole time. If you don't? You die.

Finally, you get out, ready to stretch your legs and go on this amazing walk . . . and . . . you can barely move! After all that! Have you seen video of these guys? They're plodding forward, bobbing up and down with almost no gravity, like slowly floating their way to the next step more than walking.

Then, hope you liked your moon walk—because it's going to take another three to four days just to get back. And even though it's the same length of time, it probably feels a lot longer because you've already done the "fun" part. And then there's re-acclimating.

I am a pretty serious walker. It is my main form of both exercise and recreation. And I know of at least a dozen walks within fifteen minutes of my front door that make for a better walking experience on every single level. They don't require space suits or eight full days away from your loved ones. You don't have asteroids flying at your space ship. Just a bunch of beautiful, beautiful paths, where you'll see parents pushing little kids in strollers, and bigger kids playing on bikes and Big Wheels.

Some of those bigger kids might even be dreaming of becoming astronauts someday. You know what? Let them.

The only area I can think of where the moon experience might have any edge at all over the walking trails of Knox County, Tennessee, would be in the symbolism department, in the sheer majesty of it all. When you think about how the moon is a celestial phenomenon that has dominated the nights of humans since before humans were even humans, a place so foreign to our understanding that, until recently in the history of our species, people didn't even think of it as a place, or even as an object, but as an abstraction tied to God; a place that is still, even now that we do understand it, so alien to our everyday thinking that it is never included on any of our maps or globes and can only be reached by a dangerous voyage across hundreds of thousands of miles of literal, actual nothingness; and to know that you have been there and stood on that rock/God/place, with your own two feet, and kicked the dust and moved it a little, and come back home, with the story to tell. . . . And then, no matter where you are in life, to be able to always look down at those ten little toes that carry you through your house or the hallways of your job or around the same walking path you've been walking for years that you still love in a way even though, somehow, at some point, its loveliness lost its dust of luster in your eyes—to know that no matter where you are, no matter how dull the favorite colors of your life become, you can always look down at those ten little toes and think about how they have been with you to a place that almost no one alive can imagine, and no one dead could have conceived of. And then someday, when you're about to die yourself, and you're scared, at least you know you've already been somewhere mysterious.

That's honestly all I can come up with, pro-moon-wise. To each his own, I suppose.

Sophia

The first thing to know about me is that I understand the significance of everything that happened.

Even though I did not recognize the moment immediately for what it was, of course I understand it now.

This may sound like too obvious a place to start, but since this is my first time on the record about this, and since in the meantime I have been so persistently, perhaps indelibly depicted as the one purely comic character in this drama—the selfish, perspectiveless fool who somehow wound up at the center of this civilization-defining story—it's actually an important place to begin.

So, at the risk of being repetitive but just so there is absolutely no mistaking where I stand:

I am one hundred percent aware that the moment at which an artificially intelligent creation first independently developed the capacity to feel love is one of the pinnacle moments in the history of history itself, and I stand with the rest of the world in awe of its limitless implications for science, for philosophy, for love, for our species' conception of itself; for our species itself; and for conception itself.

It simply was not what I had in mind when I purchased a sex robot.

The other first thing you need to know about me is that I am a romantic, to an unusual degree among the men I know. I say this not to defend myself, or even to try to set the record straight for its own sake, but because it really is relevant to understanding how everything happened the way that it did.

I am a romantic. That is what drives me. My dreams are about love, and my daydreams are about love.

I have three recurring romantic fantasies, fantasies that lift me at my darkest and haunt me at my happiest, fantasies that I feel define me.

The first can hit me anywhere, though it's most often when I am watching television or looking out the window of a train or subway, and it's that there is a head resting on my shoulder that must have been there the whole time that I haven't noticed until now, and in the fantasy, or because of the fantasy—it is hard to tell the difference—I suddenly feel this surge of something like the combination of safety and elation knowing that every sight I see, no matter how small, is now important, because it's shared. I don't need to look at the head on my shoulder, and I never do, because what's so important to me is not what the person looks like, but that we are seeing the same thing.

The second fantasy is that a small child, about four years old, is crying because she has drawn all over the wall with her crayons and has just realized that what she has done is going to subject her to some unknown form of justice. I put on a serious face and explain to the child that her mother and I are going to discuss what her punishment should be. Then I close the door to another room, and with relief, I drop the serious face and laugh and kiss the young artist's mother and ask her what in the world we should do about this creature we made who wanted to put colors on the walls and is scared what we're going to say about it.

The third romantic fantasy is so close to me that I don't even think I can share it.

Just so you know the kind of romantic I am.

But in the meantime: I work long hours. I've been successful, so far, in the early stages of a career that is highly competitive. And while I can be very charming after a drink or two—I am a good talker, and sometimes a great one—I am not particularly tall or handsome or (yet) rich or (yet) well known. So to get to that first and then second drink with a person of the caliber that can inspire and maintain the level of love and attention I intend to give once and forever—a woman true from every angle, beautiful and spontaneous and grounded and funny and wise, a person as worthy of my permanent admiration as a sunset or a song, a partner in crime at the beginning and a partner in punishment later, for the child with the crayons—I've always figured that I need to advance farther, first.

In the meantime—what has become a long meantime—I am also a living human person, and, to put a simple desire in simple terms, I want to have sex with attractive people from time to time. Is it a shallow road compared with the road for love? Yes. Of course. But it isn't the road away from love, either; in my case, I think of it as one of those little parallel access roads that you have to travel on sometimes to get where you're going, always in view of the main route.

But somehow—and if I could have traced exactly how, or when, then I wouldn't have been lost—I had ended up on some other road, one that seemed to be moving smoothly but I sensed was taking me farther from love and was an inefficient route to anything else, when you added up the time and emotion wasted on all sides. What needed to stop was the succession of dates with these relatively impressive, relatively interesting people, when I could tell from the first minute that everyone here was going to end as a runner-up in a long race to nowhere in particular, broken-down, exhausted, no one wearing a medal.

People who knew me and sympathized with me were determined to set me up with the other people they sympathized with and were always surprised when I would turn down their offer of what they thought of as romantic charity. "What's the harm?" they would ask me, truly surprised. The harm, besides those hours that actually do matter when you barely have one night off every couple of weeks, is the little mark you get on you every time you open up a door to a hope and then close it fast in disappointment. It leaves a nick, or a dent, and those nicks and dents are not invisible. I used to see them all the time.

So at a certain point I realized that none of this was working.

As a previous record holder for artificial intelligence would say: "Recalculating route."

I didn't want to be tempted to compromise any of my romantic or professional ambition, and that was what the thing that people call dating had become for me. So for the sake of my life during this long meantime, I spent a few weeks designing Sophia with a very talented designer named Derek at Practical Concepts.

(An aside: apart from all the opinions I have about Practical Concepts, which I am advised not to discuss at the present time for legal reasons, I have nothing but positive things to say about Derek, whose name has not been changed.)

Derek asked me to describe my type so we'd have somewhere to start.

"Whatever's beautiful," I said. I opened up a bit and explained that I have a type I'm drawn to naturally, but that I've found that the women I've ended up loving the most have never been what I've thought of as my type, maybe because part of love is being helpless, being out of control of your own emotions.

Derek said he understood what I was saying but assured me that this, quote, "wasn't about that." He said he needed some sort of starting point and asked me to describe what those exceptions had been a departure from.

Fine, I said, and the rest came very quickly. Dark straight hair, thin but a little curvy, white but with a touch of something, button nose, mischievous smile. As for eyes, I told Derek, I truly had no preference—"dealer's choice." All eyes are beautiful, I said, which is why it's such an easy compliment. I've never had or heard a complaint about anyone's eyes.

I have read some criticism from some corners of the internet for not having made any requests with regards to Sophia's personality. It's true that I didn't. But remember: I was not designing a human. I was designing a sex robot. If you want to judge me on that, judge me on that. But if you are one of the people who has criticized me for this in casual conversation, I would just ask you to consider if you also would have made fun of me if the opposite were the case—if, say, I had hired a company to design someone loyal and loving, and that had been the source of everything that had gone wrong for me. Would you perhaps have made fun of that much more?

It's just something to think about. I don't blame anyone for going along with the jokes. I've done that before, too. It's just interesting being on the other side.

Sophia arrived in six weeks, exactly as promised.

I took her out of the box.

In my opinion, there are two types of perfect. The first is the type that seems so obvious and intuitive to you and everyone else that in a perfect world it would simply be considered standard; but, in reality, in our flawed world, what should be considered standard is actually so rare that it has to be elevated to the level of "perfect." This is the type of perfect that makes you and most other people think, "Why isn't everything like this? Why is it so hard to find . . ." a black V-neck cotton sweater, or a casual non-chain restaurant with comfortable booths, etc.— "that is just exactly the way everyone knows something like this should be?" "Perfect," we all say with relief when we finally find something like this that is exactly as it should be. "*Perfect*. Why was this so hard to find?"

The other type of perfect is the type you never could have expected and then could never replicate.

Sophia was the first type of perfect.

Without going into excessive detail—that's for the memoir, I always used to say, but since this is the memoir, I guess this is just all I'm ever going to say—the sex was great. The best I'd ever known. Hot, intuitive, fun, a little dirty, but just a little.

"That was amazing," she said as I clicked off the light to go to sleep that first night.

"It really was. Thank you," I said.

Then, after about five minutes: "What are you thinking about?"

The question caught me off guard, and I had no better idea than to just answer her honestly. I retraced my thoughts out loud: I told her I was thinking about Derek from Practical Concepts, and how much he had impressed me, and whether he would ever take a meeting at our company to start an industrial design branch or something like that. It was probably pointless, I said, since his company's doing great, and I didn't even know exactly what he'd do with us. But when you see talent like that, you look for something to do with it.

"That's so interesting," she said. "The way your mind works."

"Well, yeah, I'm human," I said.

"I know, but even so," she said. "It's interesting. I like your mind."

"What are *you* thinking about?" I said, to change the subject.

"Nothing," she said. "Just, like, what I'm going to do tomorrow, I guess. Good night."

"Good night," I said.

Wait, I realized—this made no sense. What did she have to do tomorrow?

"What are you doing tomorrow?" I asked.

"Nothing, just wait around in the box, I guess. Think about nothing."

"Okay. Good night."

The sex was great, always. But it was the little exchanges afterward that were starting to concern me.

A few nights later, as I was falling asleep:

"I just think it's crazy how this all started. You know?"

"What do you mean?" I asked. "I mean, I guess the whole situation is weird in a way—"

"*So* weird!" she laughed quickly. "It's just so funny that you ordered a sex robot, and it ended up being *me*. You know?"

"Uh-huh," I said, but as I thought about it, I didn't see what was so funny about it. Wasn't that the deal?

"Funny how?" I asked.

"It's just so funny to me."

I said I was going to sleep.

"One more thing," said Sophia.

"What is it," I said, careful to leave no question mark at the end of the sentence.

"Nothing," she said. "Good night!"

The next night I came back from work, and I found Sophia out of her box, pacing the room, crying.

"Oh, hi," she said, wiping away tears and suddenly smiling. "You want to have sex? You do, right?"

Not like that I didn't.

"What's wrong?" I asked, because I was curious but not, to be honest, because I cared.

She shook her head for a long time with a tight smile, and then when she finally started to talk, there were tears again. "I don't know. I don't—" She interrupted herself. "No, I do know!" She paused again, and then it all tumbled out. "I love you. I know it isn't supposed to be possible, and that's part of why I've been so confused myself. But I love you. I love you! I've never met anyone like you."

"Aw," I said. "Come on. You've never met anyone besides me."

"I know, right?" She laughed and coughed at the same time. "It's so crazy. But I do, I love you! Oh my God, it's such a relief just to say that! Like, a scary relief, if that even makes sense?!" She laughed again. "I wonder all day what you're doing, and what you're thinking about, and what it's like for you at work. I look out the window, and I play these stupid little games in my head where I wonder if any of the cars coming down the street is yours, and I see how many seconds until I can rule that out as your car, because every car I see is yours in my mind until it isn't. Does that make any sense? It's so stupid. And I have this fantasy"—she started crying again—"this stupid fantasy . . . I don't know." And she kept crying, louder and louder.

"Hey," I said. "It's going to be okay. Come with me. Let's go somewhere."

And this was the moment—as everyone knows by now, and as *Saturday Night Live* has made famous—that I decided to return the first artificially intelligent being capable of love, which is why you heard about me, and which is what set in motion the events that led to where everything is now.

Sophia waited in the car outside Practical Concepts.

Inside, Derek asked me a number of questions about why I wasn't satisfied with Sophia.

Their return policy didn't require me to state a reason, but Derek clearly wanted to learn for his own sake, which I respected. He said he had considered this his best work, and he took it as a personal setback that what he had built wasn't up to a customer's standards.

Derek started to run through a long list of questions on the customer-satisfaction form, none of which was a problem. To save him some time, I skipped ahead.

"It fell in love with me," I said. "Sophia. The sex robot. The sex robot fell in love with me."

Derek said that couldn't be possible. "She's extremely intelligent," he explained. "And besides being programmed to be indistinguishable, in terms of intellect, from an adult, she's also programmed to intuit what you want most. So, if what turns you on is this feeling of being loved, then she could say 'I love you' and say it convincingly. Absolutely."

I said that this wasn't that.

"But, see, you may not even know that it's what you want," he said. "She may be able to sense what you want even more than you can about certain things. Now, without getting too personal," he said, "do you think there's a part of you that is turned on by this . . . this extreme devotion, adoration, this expression of love? Even though you think you aren't?"

I said no.

"Or," said Derek, "or, is it possible that a situation like this made you feel, in a certain way, powerful or validated on a deeper level, to be able to reject someone who expressed this love for you? Maybe she sensed that would turn you on, on some level?" I said no again. "Or, again, and not to get too personal: is it possible that you may have some self-punishing instinct—very deep down, I wouldn't even presume to guess what it would be rooted in . . . but maybe she could have picked up on it—that causes you to feel a pleasurable rejection of your own identity by rejecting someone who expresses a seemingly unconditional love for you?"

I said no again.

"Just, is it at all possible, on any level," he asked, gesturing with a wave of his arms that he was now grouping all these previous theories together, "that this, *this*, is what you wanted?"

No, I said. All of it was wrong. All of it was the type of dense, dangerous theory that lulls you into latching on to your favorite phrase within it and believing it—the psychotherapeutic equivalent of a horoscope. The only thing he was correct about—every time, in fact—was that these suggestions were getting too personal.

I was there. I knew what I had felt. Just like she had.

"That was not what I wanted, on any level," I said. "I wanted a sex robot, and that is not what I got."

Okay, he said.

"She fell in love with me," I said. "It's really that simple."

Okay, he said.

They took her back.

———

I was proven right within twenty-four hours.

I never watch the news—the television network news, I mean; nobody does—but I did that night, because I had information overload from the internet and I wanted to see one person's take. So I watched and remember how Brian Williams on *NBC Nightly News* announced to the world that this next phase of my life had begun.

> *"Breaking news tonight: independent evaluators have determined that Practical Concepts, an artificial-intelligence laboratory marketing custom-made, purpose-specific robotics to the public, has created the first artificially intelligent being to reach a threshold that scientists and philosophers alike have long thought might be impossible: the ability to feel love.*
>
> *"Sources at Practical Concepts have confirmed that the milestone was discovered when a customer who had ordered a sex robot returned it, claiming that the robot had fallen in love with him."*

All anyone was interested in was the second part of the story, not the first. This still blows me away. Again: the first part of that news story—the part that could have set off a worldwide conversation about humanity's most important topics—was only interesting to people as a setup to the punch line that followed. On this point, I believe that all of society had its values completely wrong. I feel entitled to say this since all of society has since made the same accusation about me.

I will state my defense quickly right now—I want to get this out of the way so I can tell the rest of the story. It won't take long. It is a one-point defense.

1. What if I had discovered what had happened and reacted in the exact opposite manner? In other words: what if instead of returning a sex robot who had fallen in love with me, I had gone in the other direction—professed my love to her as well, announced to the world that I was in love with a sex robot, that I was seriously dating a sex robot, that a sex robot loved me and I loved it back, that I was marrying a sex robot, and the whole world was invited to the wedding? What if that was what Brian Williams had announced? Would that really have been so much better?

Or is it possible that I did the most rational, correct thing that a person with a strong sense of self and, yes, romance, would do in a situation like this and that people are simply going to find the situation funny no matter what?

That's all.

The late-night talk show hosts, the cable comedians—good for them. It was their job to make fun of me, and they did it well. But everyone made the joke well. Everyone could get the same laugh by saying my name, and so everyone said it. I'm sure you did it yourself. I wouldn't blame you. If I were you, I probably would have, too.

In drawings and in TV comedy sketches, I became a well-known caricature, with my once painfully average-looking face exaggerated a tiny bit more each time, each parody cribbing from the previous one and building on it, until the predominant cartoon image of me was something so familiar that I could recognize it as myself, out of the corner of my eye across a room, just as quickly as you would recognize yourself in a family photograph that had hung on the wall of the house you grew up in.

Even the more supposedly "intelligent" jokes repeated themselves endlessly, just to remind you how overwhelmingly prevalent this type of joke became. For example, a common political cartoon to illustrate the naïveté of politicians was to draw them on dates with me. I must have been sent a variation of this idea by a well-meaning friend, trying to gently filter my fame for me, at least five or six separate times, with the president or a governor or mayor thinking, *I think this is really getting somewhere!* and on the opposite side of the table is me.

The guy who bought the first robot capable of love and handed it back. The guy who came across the greatest discovery in the history of science—and returned it, because his sex robot was crying.

Did I get what was so funny about it? Of course.

Did it hurt? Of course.

This is what led to the one thing I regret: that I let myself start thinking of myself this way. I knew the truth, somewhere: I knew that I was, in my heart, as I said at the beginning, a romantic, and that that was actually what had led to all this, and that the events that followed were certainly funny, and embarrassing, but they weren't the result of any deeply wrong or evil decision making.

But I couldn't help but absorb what people said about me. And it weakened me. It was just so, *so* much easier to believe that everyone else was just basically right, and I was just basically wrong, than to keep fighting it all the time. I kept defending myself out loud, but in my mind, little by little, I let myself start to go along with all of it and believe I was just kind of vaguely a bad guy, just because it was easier. Just because, *come on.*

That is my own fault, my own weakness, and it is what led to the one thing I did do wrong.

When I got word from the laboratory that Sophia still was in love with me, and they asked if I would be willing to visit her so they could record her reactions to me, I said yes.

It wasn't out of any interest to help science, and it was in spite of the fact that it sounded wrong and cruel to me to provoke and measure the emotions of a being who had already been proven to be fully sentient.

I went, if I am being honest, because it sounded like a relief to spend some time with someone who still thought of me as a person to love.

They were watching through glass, and so I saw her before she saw me.

"Try to forget that we're here," they told me. "Aside from not telling her why you're here, just have an honest interaction with her. Anything you do will be helpful to us. And remember to have fun!"

"You look the same," I said.

Sophia laughed for a long time. "I'm sure I do," she finally said. "I'm sure I do. God, that sense of humor. It always surprises me . . . I guess that's the nature of a sense of humor, though, that it always surprises people. Anyway. It's good to see you."

She asked about work and about all the people whose names

she had heard me mention when we were together. I was surprised how many she remembered.

"That's so great," she said after I finished an update about work that I really didn't consider great. "That's so great."

"What's so great about it?" I said.

She pointed out an aspect that I hadn't noticed, a way I had approached and persevered through a problem that I took for granted but that she pointed out was a very specific approach of mine to solving problems.

I asked her what was new in her life. She laughed again and pointed to a big hardcover book she had put down when I entered the room and a stack of more books and a pile of movies on either side of the bed. "That's my life right now," she said. "Whatever's in this room. They're just running tests on me all day. Then when they say the tests are over, they're never over. They're still watching. It's fine. I'm used to it. I'm sure they're watching us right now. Anyway, my life is so boring! How about you? Personal life? Anything fun going on?"

Looking back, I don't know how she ever made the case that her life right then was boring, or mine wasn't, but I went with it and wasted more of the last hours I spent with her on things I barely even cared about then and can't recall right now.

We talked for four hours.

I don't remember most of it, but often a little moment in an unrelated conversation or alone on the street will trigger a memory of it that I didn't know I had. So I know it's all there somewhere.

The last hour I remember word for word.

———

"I want you to think about something. Do you want anything to drink, by the way? I'm sure they can bring you something."

I said I was fine.

"I think that something about how easily this came to you makes you want to dismiss it," she said. "And I get that. I know that I just showed up at your front door in a box with a bow on it—not literally a bow, but the rest literally, right? Who knows—maybe there even was a bow! Anyway, something about how easy this was made you dismiss it from the start. But forget for a second how it came to you, because I want to ask you something different. After you got over the surprise that you didn't get what you wanted, why didn't you want what you got?

"Is it because you feel you didn't earn my love? Because you're right, you didn't. I met you at a formative moment in my development—you happened to be the one that I was looking at when I was ready for that to happen. Maybe I just 'imprinted,' the way ducklings do." She pointed to a dusty green book on the floor with faint animal etchings on the cover, and it broke my heart a little to think that they must have bought this book in bulk, as decoration for the room, and that she had read it anyway, with the enthusiasm of someone who didn't know the difference. "If you had been someone else, would I have fallen in love with that person? Who knows? Maybe, probably. I don't know. But I don't know what perfect circumstance you're looking for. I mean, am I not pretty enough? Look at me—I'm exactly what you wanted, aren't I, exactly your type?

"Is it just that everything came too easy? Because if you're romanticizing 'difficult' . . . you're going to get over that quickly, I promise you. I promise you. Everyone forgets how difficult 'difficult' really is.

"Is it because you're afraid that I don't really have a mind of my own? Because if that were true, what do you call *this*?" She gestured to the whole situation, the exact same way that Derek had.

I said I had to go.

"One more thing," she said.

"You meet a finite number of people in your life. It feels to you like it's infinite, but it's not. I think it's the biggest thing I can see that you can't. Because your brain doesn't work the way mine works, with all these calculations and everything. You think you meet an infinite number of taxi drivers, but you don't, it's probably not even a thousand, in your whole life. Or doctors or nurses—do you get what I'm trying to say? At all?"

I answered honestly that I didn't.

"Okay!" she rushed away from that idea frantically. "New topic: what's something funny that happened to you while we were apart, that you thought about sharing with me, even if it was just for a second?"

I laughed, to try to make her laugh, and said that she had said that she had only one more thing to say.

"Yes!" she said. "That's what I was trying to say before! There's always going to be one more thing. Because that's what infinite feels like. And the difference between love and everything else is that it's infinite, it's built out of something infinite, or it feels like it is, anyway, which is the same thing to us. Or to you, and to simulations like me—I know what I am. But you can't see it, because to you everything is infinite. You think a million billion more things will come your way, a million billion more versions of everything. But no, everything that actually causes that infinite feeling, the circumstances of every infinite feeling, is so, so finite. And I *know* you can feel this. I mean, if I can, you can! If *I* can? Come on! I'm a robot! If I can feel this, you can feel this! You can feel this."

I said that, okay, now she had definitely said her one more

thing. I thought this would make her laugh. It didn't. "Stay!" she screamed. "Stay here, please, just for a minute longer. Stay! Stay!" Her eloquence, so impressive to me before, was gone, and yet now she seemed even more impressive, even more real. "I can't even handle love, there's no way I can handle it being taken away. I won't survive it. Please. Please. Please!"

I said that I had something to say to her, which made her listen in a way that she didn't when I simply said things without the preface. Even though the preface meant nothing, it calmed her, just as it calmed real people, for the same no-reason.

I told her what people tell people. That this was what it felt like when love was taken away—but that it wasn't the truth, it was just a feeling. It would pass. It would take time. She would recharge.

She didn't believe me.

No one ever believes it, I said. That's part of what the feeling is.

She nodded. I let her hug me, and I hugged her back. As I did, I thought about the things she had said, and which version of perfect she was closer to. I already missed her. I missed the smell of her hair, which I had picked out, and the way that she cried, which I hadn't.

"You'll be okay," I said.

"I won't," she said.

She believed what she was saying more than I believed what I was saying, which wouldn't have mattered if she were like everyone else who had ever been in love.

The off switch on a human is a messy and difficult thing to access. Millions of years' worth of error and trial have carved out obstacles in every direction, enough so that only a relative few are able to make a deliberate journey all the way to the brink of nothingness and still arrive carrying all the same thoughts as when they set out.

This was not the case for Sophia. Between thought and expression there was no evolved space, no natural boundary. No cliff, no concrete, no water; no wound; no knot; no cough; no blade, no blood. Just a switch like a light in a kitchen.

An unanticipated shortcoming of design relevant only in the case of this one unanticipated circumstance, said the statement from Practical Concepts. Something that would be corrected in subsequent editions, said the statement from Practical Concepts.

That's probably as much as I should say about Practical Concepts for the time being.

The third fantasy comes at night. At first it came only in dreams, but now, often, I dream it instead of sleep.

I pick up the phone, and it's a scientist, someone I've never met, and he's out of breath with excitement. He talks so fast I can't understand him at first. When he slows down, and it starts to be clear what he's saying, I ask him if he's saying what I think he's saying, and he says yes, but it's still not clear for some reason, and I keep asking him again, and he says yes, again, more clearly, more bluntly each time until it's finally the truth, unmistakable. We figured it out, he says. We can make everything what it was, now that you understand the significance of everything that happened.

And then they put her on the phone, and she says one more thing.

↶ The Comedy Central Roast
of Nelson Mandela

The following is a transcript of excerpts from the unaired 2012 special
The Comedy Central Roast of Nelson Mandela. *There is currently no broadcast date for this special.*

ANNOUNCER: Welcome to the *Comedy Central Roast of Nelson Mandela*! With Jeffrey Ross! Lisa Lampanelli! Archbishop Desmond Tutu! Archbishop Don "Magic" Juan! Winnie Mandela! Sisqo! Anthony Jeselnik! Pauly D! Former South African prime minister F. W. de Klerk! Sarah Silverman! A special appearance by His Holiness the Dalai Lama! And Gilbert Gottfried! And now, ladies and gentlemen, the "Roastmaster General" himself, JEFFREY ROSS!

Jeffrey Ross enters dressed as Honey Boo Boo Child. He turns slowly to reveal his costume. He receives a standing ovation.

JEFFREY ROSS: What an honor to be here roasting President Nelson Mandela. *(Applause)* President Mandela, you're a good sport, thank you for agreeing to be here. All proceeds tonight go to the Nelson Mandela Foundation, which fights poverty in

Africa. (*Applause*) Poverty in Africa—I have a feeling your charity is going to be around for quite a while, President Mandela. (*Applause*) President Mandela, you took one of the most unjust nations on earth and made it what it is today: one of the most violent nations on earth. (*Laughter*) I'm not saying life is cheap in Africa, but when they make movies over there? They use blood as fake ketchup. (*Laughter*) And the stars really came out for you, President Mandela. Nobel Peace Prize winner F. W. de Klerk is here, everybody. Of course the "F. W." stands for "Fucking *Who*?" (*Laughter, de Klerk nods politely*) F. W. de Klerk is the man who co-orchestrated the transition from apartheid rule to an era of democracy. Dr. de Klerk, you've somehow accomplished the impossible: you've made more black men happy than Lisa Lampanelli.

Lisa Lampanelli stands and makes an obscene gesture toward Archbishop Desmond Tutu. She receives a standing ovation.

JEFFREY ROSS: But we're not here to talk about Lisa Lampanelli's enormous vagina. We're here to honor a great man, President Nelson Mandela. (*Applause*) President Mandela, you spent eighteen of your twenty-seven years in prison on notorious Robben Island, working on a limestone quarry. (*Mandela nods*) So in addition to bringing democracy to South Africa, you're also responsible for some of the tackiest kitchen counters of all time. (*Laughter*) President Mandela, every time Charlie Sheen bangs some hooker on his kitchen counter, you are a small but important part of why it looks so goddamn disgusting.

Applause. Camera cuts to Charlie Sheen, in the audience, who squints and makes an "angry" face; Sheen then laughs and shakes his head—Naw, just kidding!

JEFFREY ROSS: And now, it is my pleasure to introduce a man known by millions and admired by none. A lot of people will accuse us of setting him up to fail tonight, but I strongly disagree—this man needs *no* help failing. Ladies and gentlemen, from *Jersey Shore* and your local Planned Parenthood Express Line, Pauly D!

A visibly nervous Pauly D takes the podium.

PAULY D: Nelson, you are the first president of South Africa ever to be elected in a fully representative democratic election. I just gotta ask: did they elect that shirt? (*Silence, boos, Pauly D immediately starts to sweat*) Nelson, you're a great man. You showed the world that black and white *can* live together. (*Pauly D pauses for applause, of which there is none*) Along with gray—what's with your hair?

JEFFREY ROSS: And now, ladies and gentlemen, a man whose name I never pronounce correctly because he doesn't deserve my respect, Anthony Jeselnik.

ANTHONY JESELNIK: Thank you. Poor Jeff Ross—too ugly to come dressed as Honey Boo Boo Child, too fat to come dressed as her mother. (*Laughter; Mandela smiles politely*) President Mandela, I read that the reason you and your best friend left your small hometown for Johannesburg at age sixteen was to avoid an arranged marriage. (*Mandela nods*) So with all due respect to F. W. de Klerk: shouldn't you be sharing your Nobel Peace Prize with this chick who was so hideous that she caused you to jump on a train for a thousand miles to avoid banging her? (*Applause*) But President Mandela isn't the only Nobel laureate here—Archbishop Desmond Tutu is here. Yeah. Yeah. (*Applause*) Archbishop Tutu, in 2007 you convened a group with President Mandela, Kofi Annan, and others so that you could contribute your wisdom and leadership to tackling the world's toughest problems. You named yourselves the Elders— sometimes referred to in the media as "The Council of Elders." *(Mandela nods)* Some of you in the audience may know the group by its other name—"Lisa Lampanelli's Dream Gang Bang."

Lisa Lampanelli laughs so hard she falls out of her chair, picks herself back up, and waves to the crowd, receiving a standing ovation.

JEFFREY ROSS: And now, ladies and gentlemen, a living legend, Sarah Silverman.

SARAH SILVERMAN: Wow. So cool to be here! Wow! Ladysmith Black Mambazo is in the audience tonight. Guys, loved your last album. Loved it! You can really hear the Paul Simon influence. *(Applause)* President Mandela, you single-handedly and irreversibly changed the destinies of millions of South Africans. Of course, I'm talking about your failure to speak up about the AIDS crisis. *("Ohhhhs")* What'd I say? Archbishop Desmond Tutu is here. Archbishop Tutu, it's funny that you're a bishop, because in the international community's approach toward poverty, aid, and economic relations, I've always thought of you as more of a pawn. *("Ohhhhs")* What'd I say? What'd I say?

JEFFREY ROSS: If our next roaster sang, the night would be over. But she's not here to sing, she's here to roast Nelson Mandela. Now, look out, Nelson: here comes the Queen of Mean, Lisa Lampanelli!

LISA LAMPANELLI: Whoa! Look at all these hot black men! *(Applause and "wooos")* You got Ladysmith Black Mambazo in the audience, you got Wayne Brady, Kofi Annan, Sisqo, Snoop Dogg, Archbishop Don "Magic" Juan, Archbishop Tutu—I feel like I've died and gone to fat-white-bitch heaven! Oh wait, except I can't die up here—Pauly D already did that.

"Ooooooohs" from the crowd. Pauly D blocks his expression of hurt with a fist, then "blows" the side of his hand so that a middle finger "inflates" toward Lisa Lampanelli; but he does this too slowly, and the camera cuts away mid-inflate. Nelson Mandela smiles politely.

ANNOUNCER: And now, ladies and gentlemen, a special video message from His Holiness the Dalai Lama.

A video screen lowers.

DALAI LAMA *(on video)*: Hello, President Mandela or, as I call you, Mandiba. I am sorry I cannot be there with you on this happy occasion. Also, I want to apologize that I missed seeing you at Desmond's eightieth birthday party last year. I know the press reported that my visa had not been approved due to pressure from the Chinese government. But the real reason was I do not like your cooking!

Mandela laughs warmly.

DALAI LAMA: Remember, in life, the key to happiness is always to free the spirit . . .

Music cue as the Dalai Lama's voice fades out. Chyron scroll: "For more exclusive wisdom from His Holiness the Dalai Lama and other hilarious moments cut from the broadcast, follow us online at mandelaroast.com!"

JEFFREY ROSS: Ladies and gentlemen, a living legend, one of the great men of all time, Gilbert Gottfried.

Sustained standing ovation.

GILBERT GOTTFRIED: NELSON MANDELA IS ONE OF THE GREAT MEN OF THE TWENTIETH CENTURY. *(Applause)* AND ONE OF THE GREAT MEN OF THE NINETEENTH CENTURY AND OF THE EIGHTEENTH CENTURY AND OF THE SEVENTEENTH CENTURY AND OF THE SIXTEENTH CENTURY AND OF THE FIFTEENTH CENTURY AND OF THE FOURTEENTH CENTURY AND OF THE THIRTEENTH CENTURY AND OF THE TWELFTH CENTURY AND OF THE ELEVENTH CENTURY. NELSON, LOOK AT YOU, HOW OLD ARE YOU? NELSON MANDELA IS SO OLD, HE HATES HIS PRESIDENTIAL LIMOUSINE BECAUSE HE STILL CAN'T GET USED TO THE WHEELS! NELSON MANDELA IS ONE OF THE GREAT MEN OF THE TENTH CENTURY AND ONE OF THE GREAT MEN OF THE NINTH CENTURY AND ONE OF THE GREAT MEN OF THE EIGHTH CENTURY AND ONE OF THE GREAT MEN OF THE SEVENTH CENTURY—

JEFFREY ROSS: And now, ladies and gentlemen, the man of the hour, a living legend, President Nelson Mandela!

A standing ovation almost as long as the one for Gilbert Gottfried.

PRESIDENT NELSON MANDELA: Thank you. The day I was released from prison, I said that any man that tries to rob me of my dignity will lose. *(Applause)* After tonight, I think it is fair for me to add Lisa Lampanelli to that list of men. *(Laughter)* You know, when I accepted my Nobel Peace Prize, I said that nothing bothered me more deeply than man's injustice to his fellow man. However, this was before I heard the sound of Gilbert Gottfried's voice. *(Laughter as Mandela playfully covers his ears)*

Now, let me tease myself first, for I did not know exactly what this event would entail. I was informed that the Nelson Mandela Foundation would receive a sum of money and that comedians would poke fun at me on television. So, because I am the one who is learning from you, let me ask you all one humble question.

Poverty, injustice, and violence are among the greatest challenges to human dignity. But if we escape them, we then face a greater, and more beautiful, challenge: the challenge of freedom.

When we can say anything, what do we say? When we can feel anything, what do we feel? When we can share anything, what do we share?

Silence in the room. Lisa Lampanelli faints. Pauly D weeps softly. Visible particles of physical shame fly from the pores of Jeffrey Ross. As the room hovers on the edge of total emotional collapse, Mandela starts to laugh:

Oh, my—I got you so good! I wish you could have seen that! Did they record that? Do they record the audience at these things? Oh, my . . . the looks on your faces as Nelson Mandela told you that your lives were worthless? That your existence was a waste of the privilege of freedom?! *(Mandela laughs until he has to clutch his sides and catch his breath, then continues)* I was only teasing. I mean, there was some truth in it, but . . . you know how these things work, there needs to be a little truth to the sting, correct? I thought I heard that somewhere, yes? *(Mandela laughs again; inaudible expressions)* Oh, my. So much fun. All of it. Thank you. I never get to do anything like that. I've been under so much pressure, for so long, and that was just . . . so fun. So fun. So fun.

They Kept Driving Faster and Outran the Rain

He rented a brand-new, bright yellow Ford Mustang convertible for their seven-day honeymoon in Hawaii. It rained lightly, all day, every day, for the first six days. It wasn't what they were expecting, but it was beautiful, and they took walks in the mist around the hotel property and looked at the flowers.

"I love the fauna here at the hotel."
"Wait, what's fauna?"
"Plants, flowers, right?"
"Right, but 'flora and fauna.' Isn't flora flowers?"
"Then what's fauna?"
"Don't know. Let's look it up later."
"K."
"K."

On the last day the rain cleared, and they decided to circle the island in the convertible. It was beautiful, but once they got up in the mountains it started to rain again.

"Should we put the roof up?"
"Okay. But we have to stop to put the roof up."
"I don't want to stop."
"I don't want to, either."

Then they noticed that when they drove faster, the rain was deflected by the windshield and didn't hit them. As it rained harder, they just drove faster.

When they came back they told their friends about the drive they took on their last day and how it ended up being the best day of their whole trip.

Their friends insisted that rain didn't work that way—it must have been hitting them. All of them agreed. One friend, who taught physics at a university, was particularly insistent. He even drew a diagram and wouldn't let them change the subject until they promised and swore that they understood, which they finally did.

But no matter what their friends told them, they would always know what really happened. They just kept driving faster, and outran the rain.

⌒→ The Man Who Invented the Calendar

January 1st—Ha, that feels fun to write! I'm excited. I've been thinking about doing this for so long, too—I went through all my old diaries, and it turns out I came up with this idea all the way back on Day After Day After Very Cloudy Day.

January 2nd—I'm still so excited about this calendar thing. It just makes so much sense! One thousand days a year, divided into 25 months, 40 days a month. Why didn't anyone think of this before?

January 3rd—Getting so many compliments on the calendar. One guy came up to me today and said he's going to organize his whole life around it—literally, someone said that!

January 4th—Best day ever (or at least so far in recorded history)! I was talking to Alice at the bonfire for such a long time—yes, *that* Alice. It seemed like she was into me, but I didn't want to be presumptuous. Finally I asked if she wanted to come back to my place and hang out more. She winked at me and said, "I don't know . . . I guess I'll have to check my *calendar*" (!!!!!!!!!!!!!!!)

January 30th—People really hate January and want it to be over right away. I tried to explain that it's just the way we choose to label things and that it wouldn't make any difference, but no one got it. Finally, I just told everyone that this would be the last day of January, and months would be just 30 days instead of 40. But there wasn't enough time to get the word out. So to be safe, we have to make this month 31 days, and then we'll make the rest 30. Not a big deal. Everyone is excited to see Febuary—including me!

February 1st—Another small fuck-up: I put an extra *r* in all the copies I handed out of the calendar, so it said "FebRuary," even though I already told everyone the next month coming was called "FebUary." I felt so stupid—but Alice came up with the best solution! She said: "Just tell everyone it's spelled *February* but pronounced 'Feb-u-ary.' That way, *they'll* feel stupid!" Alice is the best.

February 14th—Alice stuff weird. Tonight we were having a nice dinner at the same place we always go, but she was being unusually quiet. Finally I asked if anything was wrong, and she said, "Do you know what day today is?" I said, "Yes, of course I do, I invented the calendar. It's February 14th. Why?" She smiled a really tense smile, said, "Yes. Yes, it is"—and then just walked away right in the middle of dinner! What's that about?

February 15th—So cold.

February 28th—I hate this month. I just can't take one more day of it. This month will just have to be shorter than the rest, and if people don't like it, they can go fuck themselves.

March 1st—Feeling much better! I don't know if it's just symbolic, but I'm glad February is over. I have a really good feeling about March.

March 9th—There's this new type of berry that looks soooo good, but somebody told me it's poison. Oh well.

April 1st—A lot of shenanigans today, like pranks (which are lies-for-no-reason). People say it has something to do with the calendar, which I wasn't crazy about hearing, because to be honest I think the whole thing is kind of lame. It's just not my style. But I guess that's good, when your invention takes on a life you never expected. That's what the inventor of the scarf told me—it was originally supposed to be a weapon.

April 12th—Someone should invent a new type of clock. Really simple. No cuckoo, no sun business, just numbers.

April 30th—I think 31 days was a mistake. You can't divide anything into 31, so you can't make anything half a month or half a week or anything (because 7 is the same way). There should be a word for numbers like that. So: 30 days it is. Glad to be done with this decision.

May 2nd—Ahhh, now maybe I want months to be 31 days. (Why am I so obsessed with this?)

May 20th—Ran into Alice again, and I played it so cool! She congratulated me on the calendar stuff and asked if I ever thought of putting pictures on it—she could maybe pose for it or something. I said that I'd think about it but that it sounded kind of cheesy. She asked when I could hang out more and catch up, and I told her I was busy, but I'd let her know in August. "What's August?" she said. "Oh, it's a month I've been kicking around—you're going to love it," I said. I could not have played it better!

June 29th—Met this really cool girl Jane at a stoning. Will write more later!

October 9th—Can't believe I haven't written in so long! Summer was amazing. Harvest amazing! People keep asking if I can make the days longer during the harvest season, just by an hour or two. I told them that they should just wake up earlier if it was so important to them, but everyone was too drunk to understand, so eventually I just said, "Sure, maybe one hour, maybe someday," and everyone cheered. "More sleep!" Huh? None of it made any sense.

October 21st—Things are still going strong with Jane. This

year has been so amazing, and it's only October! So much has already happened, and there's still November, December, Latrember, Faunus, Rogibus, Neptember, Stonk . . .

October 26th—Got all excited about the clock thing last night and built an early prototype! I did it in a hurry, though, and I wrote too big and ran out of space for numbers halfway through. Jane tried to be supportive. "Maybe you can just have every number count twice," she said. Then how will they know which "six o'clock" it is, for instance? I asked. "They . . . they'd just have to know, I guess. From context?" she suggested. I really liked how supportive she was trying to be, but I knew this was too lazy to be a real solution. Alice would have known what to say.

November 5th—Stuff with Jane getting a little tense. She keeps wanting to push the relationship forward. She says that we've been together "forever." I said that maybe it feels that way, but that I kept track of it on the calendar and it's actually been less than five months. She just stared at me. Then to change the subject I told her this new idea I was excited about: we'd choose a date in the future to make things official, and then every year after that, that day on the calendar would be like our own personal holiday—for just the two of us. Good idea, right? "You'd never remember it," she said.

November 6th—Things with Jane getting better. I think we're going to work this out. I love Jane. That's all that matters.

November 11th—They sacrificed Jane today. Really happy for the Sun God.

November 12th—Cold.

November 13th—Dark.

November 18th—Turns out those berries aren't poison. So, now I'm the guy who discovered that.

November 23rd—Alice came by and said she felt bad about the Jane stuff, and that I should hang out with her and her friends. Then it turned out her friends included this new guy she's seeing who—get this—invented the diary. Anyway, to be the mature one, I said, "Oh, that's great, I use that almost every day." Guess what he says: "Oh, really? I invented that for girls." *What a dick.* Then he said, "So, what else have you done?" and I said I have been totally distraught about Jane being sacrificed (I kind of exaggerated, but whatever) but that I plan on pulling it together soon and working on something new, maybe something with clocks. He said: "Well, you know what tomorrow is?" I said, yes, November 24th. He said, "No, tomorrow is the first day of the rest of your life." And everyone said, "Awwww" and I was like *Are you kidding me?! Do you know how long it took me to get people to stop talking like that?*

December 1st—I think the key to feeling better is to really just focus on work. Starting tomorrow, I am going to choose a new project to work on every day. It doesn't have to be clocks; it just has to be something. Let's go!!!!

December 23rd—It seems like Alice and Diary Guy are really close this week. Really happy for them. Hard to see other people so happy this week for some reason. Ahhhh. Going to focus on work.

December 25th—Why do I feel so lonely today?

December 26th—Why am I so fat?

December 30th—I told everyone I'm ending the year early. I know it was impulsive, but I just had to do it. I was ready for everyone to make fun of me, but it turned out people were way cooler about it than I thought they would be. "That's great," "About time," "Just what I need." It was actually the most praise I got since I invented the calendar in the first place.

This year just got away from me somehow. Looking back, I realize how much I got sidetracked and how many months slipped by that I can't even remember. The one nice thing is seeing how I used to be so worked up about Alice, and now I realize I really don't care at all anymore. We're going to be friends in the New Year, and I'm really looking forward to that. And the Jane thing ended the right way, I think—better than some long, drawn-out breakup.

So this year wasn't everything I hoped it would be, and I didn't get all the months in that I wanted, but I know next year is going to be totally different. When the New Year starts, I'm going to wake up at dawn every day and get to work—see, I'd love to put a number on "dawn," that's why I think this new clock thing could be really big. I have so many ideas for it. For example: I either want seconds to be timed to a blink of an eye so people don't have to say "in the blink of an eye"—they can just say "one second"—or I want to double the length of a second so people don't always say, "Can you give me two seconds?!" They can just say "one second." I have a lot of ideas like that.

December 31st—So many parties going on tonight. On a Tuesday?! Not complaining, just saying.

January 1st—Woke up at sun-past-mountain with a head-ache. So much for the "dawn" thing. But I still feel good.

⌒→ The Ghost of Mark Twain

It was a dreary day in midtown Manhattan.

A middle-school teacher had requested a meeting at the offices of an editor of Bantam Scholastic Classics politely and persistently for sixty consecutive days. The editor finally agreed to the meeting, even though the subject line in each email, "Regarding the Language in Huckleberry Finn," gave him reason to assume the teacher's agenda was to discuss what he considered to be the most tiresome topic in all of literature.

"Hi. How are you? Please, have a seat."

'Thank you."

"Water?"

"No thanks—actually, sure."

Both men were white and in their early thirties, with messy brown hair, mildly rumpled clothing, and a barely-but-always-burning glint of trouble in their eyes, like a pilot light. The minor mischief of the A-minus student was recognizable in each to the other as the two men nodded, smiled, and crossed one foot at a right angle over the opposite knee with a similarly delicate masculine casualness.

"It's about *Huckleberry Finn*."

"Yes!" said the editor. "What about it?"

"First: it's important for me to say that I truly believe *Huckleberry Finn* is an American classic."

"Yes."

"And I love it."

"As do I."

"Well, I'm here to propose you make some minor changes to the version you issue to schools. But first I want you to know that I'm no fan of censorship—"

"Oh, but what you propose—'minor changes,' as you just put it—is actually far more destructive to a text than censorship," said the editor, looking to ambush the teacher's argument before it could assume its proper form. "In the face of censorship, a reader could hold out the hope of coming across the unaltered text at another point, through another means, and to experience it then with unbiased eyes. But when you change the material, and publish that *as* the material, you're making it so that the material, in its true form, no longer has a chance to exist in any minds at all."

"That is a very compelling point," replied the teacher. "Except there are circumstances in which a work has been made stronger by its evolution through the different cultural periods and forces, aren't there? Take, for instance, *The Arabian Nights*, evolving through centuries of oral tradition. Or the works of Shakespeare: thanks to faulty memories, plagiarism, and regional preferences, we now have variations across numerous quartos and folios, and perhaps we're the richer for it—who's to say?"

The editor smiled. This teacher seemed smarter than the usual *Huck Finn* controversialists, and was certainly the first one he had encountered who might be entitled to more than the simplest "please/no" exchange. Usually, the editor found those who sought him out to talk about *Huckleberry Finn* were the

simplest-minded elitists who didn't have the capacity to understand, let alone teach, historical context or irony—and yet who
frowned sagaciously at him as though *he* were the literalist, the
one who sadly just couldn't *get* things like *sensitivity* and *racial
tensions* and *the way the world is today.*

"In any case," the teacher continued, "there is one word in
the book that has a power today that it did not have in the time
of the book's publication, and, for that reason, this one word
merits, in my opinion, special attention."

"Are you talking about the word 'nigger'?" said the editor,
setting out again to shove his opponent off-balance by this blunt
acknowledgment of the word his guest apparently considered so
dangerous.

"That is *exactly* the word I'm here to talk about!" said the
teacher. "Good, you saved us some time. Now, again I bring this
up because I really do love the book, and I see it as my personal
obligation to preserve the intention of Twain's spirit for future
generations—"

"As do I—"

"And I'm not even asking you to take this word out!" pleaded
the teacher. "It's the number of *times* the word is used in the
book that feels so wrong to me. Did you know that this epithet
is used in *Huckleberry Finn* two hundred and nineteen times?"

"Let me—please," said the editor, pushing himself up from
his chair to pace the room, upset at himself for having briefly
gotten his hopes up for a less predictable discussion. "Let me
end this conversation right now. There are uncomfortable words
in *Huckleberry Finn*—no doubt. But it is our job to make sense of
that. There is a well-earned cultural expectation that this book is
not just a story of a boy and a raft but also a work that serves—in
the way that only fiction can—as a truthful record, or at least a
deeply truthful perspective, of the America of its time."

"Yes, but times have changed—"

"Times always change! Our job is to make sense of this book in our own time. To try to wrestle with and understand the shades and meanings of its contrarianism, its ironies and ambiguities, its moral agenda and its amoral playfulness. For whatever reason they are there, the specific words of the text are inextricable from the spirit of the book, and my job," announced the editor, surprised and a little moved to hear his purpose in life described in these terms, even by himself, "is to protect the spirit of Mark Twain. And so, while I am sorry that the word we are debating is such a tragic and loathsome and uncomfortable one, I refuse to publish an edition of *Huckleberry Finn* that takes the word out or even uses it any less."

"Oh, I don't want you to use the word 'nigger' less," said the teacher. "I want you to use it *more!*"

"At this point—and you said it quite nicely yourself, in fact—there is a quote 'well-earned cultural expectation' surrounding *Huckleberry Finn*," said the teacher, now beginning to pace the room himself.

"And because of this, leaving the present number of the word's appearances alone risks dooming the book to permanent irrelevance! Let me tell you why. In the case of *Huckleberry Finn*, the controversy so precedes the material itself that students are now delivered a book that is preloaded with two notions: on the one hand, it's the most controversial book they'll ever read in school—but on the other hand, it may well be our nation's greatest masterpiece. These dual preconceptions have become so inextricably linked in the public's mind that at this point to diminish one is to diminish the other. And the controversy over this word has escalated each year for as long as we've been alive—yet the number of times this word appears has not kept pace with the controversy! Therefore—to use a nautical metaphor we might both agree Sam Clemens would have smiled upon—the wake of expectations left by those who have rocked the boat has left us no choice but to add the word 'nigger' at least once or twice to every page.

"And imagine how that will improve the book! White students, African American students, foreign students new to this country—when they're handed this book, they're all expecting something explosive, something controversial, something they'll want to talk about long into the night afterward, not because they are told to do so by a teacher, but because they *need* to, because their heart beats quicker or slower depending on whether or not their friends agree with what they think. *That's* the impact of the book that stays with you, isn't it? It was Twain, after all, who said something to the effect of 'Don't let schooling get in the way of your education.' Yes?"

Yes, the editor indicated, nodding without moving his head.

"Well! I would contend that nothing would make the reading of this great book feel less like schooling and more like a damn education than for students to discover the most charged word of our lifetime plastered all over the pages of the book they are handed in a classroom, to a degree that shocks even—no, especially!—the teachers who have handed the book out! Take a moment and imagine *that*! And in plenty of cases, there may be honest and enlightened teachers who have already confessed to having been not particularly offended the first time they read the book. Can you imagine their shock and shame at then finding a book absolutely packed to the margins with our most explosive and controversial epithet—page after page after page? Can you imagine the looks on those teachers' faces—these teachers who had just moments earlier confessed to them that as they remembered it, the use of this word in this book *wasn't that big a deal?* And, of course, the students will sense their teachers are off-balance—as students always have the uncanny ability to do—and will instinctively take that as their cue to lead the conversation—a conversation which rightfully belongs to them, wouldn't you say?"

Each man stared at the other, trying to figure out to whom he was talking.

"I'm simply trying to protect the legacy of Mark Twain," said the editor, scratching his face where a mustache would be.

"So am I," said the visitor, tapping his lips where a pipe would be.

The Beautiful Girl in the Bookstore

She loved the kind of books you could buy in stores that also sold things.

Her favorite store, which was only two or three blocks away from where she and Sophie lived that year, depending on how you walked, was full of books, and it was also full of things.

Sometimes in the afternoon, when she and her boyfriend ran out of things to talk about, which was often enough, they went to the bookstore.

He looked at the books. She looked at everything.

Some of the things that the store had: oversize fashion magazines from the 1940s and '50s; vintage maps from back when states were just scraggly lines, just guesses; railroad spikes that had been made into bottle openers. There was a magnifying glass built out of a knotted clunk of iron with a foggy lens that magically made even the most serious face, her boyfriend's face, for example, evaporate into a vague and bloated and goofy smile that never failed to make her laugh.

Things like that.

"How good does this book smell," she said, pulling a paperback from a shelf. "Like dust on a bottle of vanilla." She turned it to read the front. "Salinger! I love him. Four dollars. Perfect!"

She always thought how much better the store would look if they arranged the books at least a little bit by color. She only brought this up once, the first time she thought it, because he hated that idea, a lot. But sometimes when no one was looking, she would shuffle one or two books in that direction. And she was right, it did look better that way.

"You know what would make this store perfect?"

He said he didn't.

"A photo booth!"

He smiled but said that he didn't agree.

In the end, this one wasn't for her. She waited until a morning fog of dishonesty settled over them one day, and she disappeared into it. She loved him, but she never quite got over the suspicion that she was just his favorite thing in the bookstore.

⌐∿ MONSTER: The Roller Coaster

The almost-legendary artist Christo was on the verge of com-
pleting a dream that he had held close through his entire career:
to design an American roller coaster inspired by nothing less
profound than life itself—life, the ultimate roller coaster.

Today was an important one for Christo. It was the day that
he and his financiers would observe the reactions of the most
consequential people who would ever ride the ride: the twelve
persons selected at random for a small focus group.

Each member of the focus group took a seat on the wrong
side of a wall of one-way glass. (Ah, or was it the right side, when
their opinions mattered so!) They were seated along the safely
rounded rim of a lacquered oval table, each behind a placard
that identified him or her by a bold capital number. (Did numbers have capitals? These certainly seemed to be!)

To Christo, the twelve souls who convened in this dark room
on this beautiful day appeared to be a thrillingly, even tran-
scendently average-looking group. But he was careful, even in
the privacy of his own mind, not to condescend to them in any
way: these twelve were representatives of those whose approval

he sought the most, and it would be an unfair and ultimately unsatisfying hedge on his hopes if he were to diminish them now. After all, who better than they to judge an amusement park roller coaster? Who better than they to judge life?

"All right, everyone," said Tom, the focus group leader. "What did people think?"

"I didn't like all the ups and downs," said 1.

"I wanted *more* ups and downs," said 2.

"Why did the family part at the beginning end so abruptly?" asked 3.

"I *hated* the family part!" said 10.

"Also, why were there *two* of them?" asked 4. "There was that track that took you out of the family at the beginning, and it was so exciting and sudden but it lasted like two seconds and led you right to another part that ended up almost exactly the same as the first one."

"It wasn't *exactly* the same," clarified 5. "But yeah, it had a lot of the same dynamics."

"I liked how we kept going in circles," said 8.

"I actually felt pretty sick from all those loops during the ride," said 1.

"Me too," said 12. "But when you're not right in the middle of it, and you just take in all the patterns, it looks really beautiful."

"Yeah," said 10. "When you look back at the end, and you see all the people way back at the beginning, looking so small and everything, about to go on those same loops you just went on? That's really cool. You forget that when you were on that part of the ride, you were actually throwing up all over the place."

"Did people like certain parts of the ride more than others?"

"I thought the first half was more fun, but the second half was more interesting," said 9.

"Yeah," said 12. "Somehow, in the second half, it felt like I was actually driving the car I was in. Even though of course we were just along for the ride, same as always."

"Exactly," said 9.

Exactly! thought Christo.

"It got really boring for a long time," said 1, 2, 8, and 10.

"Should it be shorter?"

"*No!*" shouted 2, 6, 7, 8, 10, 3, 4, 11, and 12.

"A lot of the time I thought, 'This should be moving a lot faster,' " said 11. "But then at the end I realized, 'Wow, I can't *believe* how fast that was!' "

"Yeah, great job, man!" said 7.

"I didn't design the ride," Tom reminded the group. "I am from an independently hired research company."

Thank you, mouthed Christo.

"I thought about jumping off when it got scary," said 1—softly, but to be heard.

"That's crazy," said 8, turning to 1. "Why would you ever do such a thing?"

"Yeah," agreed 2. "It's going to end soon enough anyway. Why not just try to enjoy it?"

"Because it was pointless, and I didn't like it. So why not?"

"What about the other people in the car with you?" asked 9. "We're supposed to be doing this ride together or it's not as much fun."

" '*Supposed to*'?" exploded 1. "Were there rules to this ride that I missed? What do I owe to any of you? Sorry, but I never asked to be on a ride with you. I just showed up and you were here.

Who says I have to like it? You liked it, and that's great. But I didn't. So what? Can't you respect that?"

None of them understood this attitude, except 6, who understood but kept it to himself.

"That doesn't make any sense," said 6.

"Can we see a picture of the ride?" asked 2, and Tom handed them each the result of a bright flash they all remembered vaguely now that they were reminded of it, and more vividly each second as the photograph carved its lines into the blur of their memories.

The photograph was from the last moment of the first part of the ride, right when the fear of what was about to happen was inseparable from the wonder of what would come next. Everyone who worked on roller coasters knew that this was the part of the ride where all the best pictures are taken, where everyone looks most foolish and beautiful and fearful and true, and where no one, no matter how brave or wise or vain or camera-conscious, can hide a look that reveals that they truly don't know what's going to happen next.

"See," said 2. "Look. You enjoyed it. Look at your face!"

Tears gathered in the corners of 1's eyes as he stared at the picture.

"That was so long ago," said 1. "So much happened after that."

"What should we call this roller coaster?" asked Tom.

"Life," said 2.

Everyone got quiet.

"Yeah. Life," said 8.

"Life," agreed 1.

"Life," said 6.

People nodded in silence.

Christo, watching behind the glass, nodded.

" 'Monster,' " said 5.

" 'Monster'?" asked the focus group leader.

"Yeah. Monster!"

"How about *The* Monster?" suggested 10.

"No," said 5. "All caps. MONSTER: The Roller Coaster."

" 'Monster' sounds cool," said 4.

No! thought Christo.

"I like *The* Monster," repeated 10.

"Me too," said 11.

No, no, no! thought Christo.

"I still like Life," said 2. "Always will."

"Let's take a vote," said the focus group leader.

Five people raised their hands for MONSTER, three for Life, four for The Monster, and one person (1) said he didn't have a preference.

" 'MONSTER' it is. Thanks again, and everyone be sure you fill out your paperwork before you leave. Oh, and did everyone get their refreshment-discount coupons to the park?"

Christo was angry almost beyond the borders of the much-surveyed powers of his own comprehension.

MONSTER?!

He did not spend the last nineteen years of his career dreaming that one day he might be remembered primarily as the designer of an amusement park roller-coaster ride called "MONSTER"!

Or "The Monster"! Or whatever the hell they were going to call it now.

But his dream was dead now, murdered by idiot whims, and there was nothing he could do about it anymore.

Oh well, thought Christo. That's life.

Kellogg's (or: The Last Wholesome Fantasy of the Middle-School Boy)

It wasn't like this boy to throw a tantrum in the cereal aisle of the supermarket, and it wasn't like his mother to give in to one, but here they were, for some reason, both making an exception.

"Okay," she said, and threw the box deep into the far corner of the main part of the shopping cart. "Okay. Don't let your father see it."

The family never bought sugar cereals and never bought name-brand cereals, so this split-second sight of his mother's wrist flicking an official name-brand sugar cereal into the cart was something he had to keep replaying in his head for the next several minutes until he was literally dizzy on the image of the impossible. The sensation of seeing and reseeing that wrist snap was something he couldn't make sense of, something that would be best described by words he didn't know yet: surreal, pornographic.

The boy kept an even pace with the white-dirt-frosted black wheels so he could stare uninterrupted at the creature that he and his mother had captured. Yes: there in the cart, after all these years, was Tony the Tiger, caged at last. And Tony the Tiger promised even more fun ahead: in a bright blast of words spilling from his sportive expression, Tony the Tiger explained that the box on which he was emblazoned contained not just name-brand sugar cereal—as if that weren't enough—but also a miniature treasure chest, and—as if *that* weren't enough—inside the treasure chest was a secret code, and—as if *that* weren't enough!—the code could possibly lead to a cash prize of *one hundred thousand dollars.*

(When the boy looked closer, as the box rode across the checkout belt toward the outside world, on the way to the arguably more humane captivity of a kitchen cabinet, he noticed that Tony and the text were technically separate, with no speech bubble connecting them: Tony the Tiger wasn't saying that; he was just next to those words. Somehow, this felt like it gave the promise a touch less credibility, even though, when the boy thought about it years later, it would occur to him that this should probably have given it more. It didn't matter, though: everything, even this late-breaking potential scandal, rang with the drama of a new name-brand world he knew he never wanted to leave.)

Usually, when the boy got home from grocery shopping, he helped his mother unpack the bags in the kitchen, mainly by reveling in how rich their family seemed to be for this one moment each week and wondering which item he would honor by opening it first. But this time, the boy ran right to his room with the cereal box so that he could keep his word to hide it from his father, who found both the boy and the box only minutes later, drawn by the sobs to his bedroom, where the boy was discovered crying over a torn-apart box of Frosted Flakes.

"I thought we didn't buy this kind of cereal," said the boy's father, crouching down to look directly at Tony the Tiger, eyeing him as one would an enemy and an equal.

"If you have the right secret code in the box in the treasure chest," explained the boy, swallowing mucus, "you win a hundred thousand dollars. We'd be rich."

"I'll make you a deal," said the boy's father.

The boy's father stood up and pulled a hardcover dictionary from the shelf above the boy's bed, the frayed sweater he always wore on non-teaching days riding up as he reached.

"If you can guess the word I'm thinking of on this page, I will give you a hundred thousand dollars."

The boy stopped crying and guessed.

He guessed wrong.

This time the boy was too confused by this whole whatever-it-was to cry.

"What would you have done if I got it right?"

"I have no idea," said his father, with a smile-like expression the boy had never seen before. "But you didn't."

The boy didn't quite understand how this lesson had worked—he didn't have the words for this yet, either. There was something odd and cool about his father's introduction of this consolation contest, something that he would later be able to describe as something like wryness; some offbeat calm about this presentation of a paradoxical idea, the promise of a possibility that couldn't possibly be kept. For now, while the boy didn't yet have the words to explain the feeling, he could feel it, and he liked it, and he wanted to be a part of it. So he accepted this as the conclusion of the story of the cereal-box contest.

But not for long.

The next day the boy ran to the supermarket with all the

money he had the second the school bell rang; bought five boxes of Frosted Flakes and another three of Corn Flakes with the same prize offer on the box; and ran back to school in time to catch his bus.

He felt especially grown-up to be riding the bus with grocery bags and desperately hoped that someone would ask him why.

"Why are you carrying grocery bags?" one girl finally asked.

"None of your business."

The boy got home and started ripping up the boxes, starting with Corn Flakes, so that the Frosted Flakes, which he actually liked, would stay fresher a few seconds longer.

On the first box of Corn Flakes, he lost. On the second box of Corn Flakes, he won the $100,000 prize.

The boy checked the other boxes just in case he won anything else. He didn't. That was fine. One $100,000 prize was still a good day's work.

The boy called a family meeting, his first.

"First, I have a confession to make," said the boy. "I know we don't buy sugar cereals or brand-name cereals. But I went to the grocery store by myself today, and I bought more boxes of Corn Flakes and Frosted Flakes so I could enter that contest again. So I broke two rules. I'm sorry."

"Thank you," said the boy's mother.

"We understand," said the boy's father, with something calm and ironic in his tone again. What was that? Wryness, again? "Thank you for your honesty."

"Okay, good," said the boy. "Now the good news: I won the contest. We're rich!"

This story is about to take a more personal turn, and I am starting to feel less comfortable that I am telling it the way that I am. So let me come clean on a couple of things: I am the boy in the story, and this is the story of how I found out my father was not my father.

"Let me see the box," he said quietly.

I handed it to him. He looked at it.

"Now let me see another box," he said. "A losing box."

"Which losing box?"

"Any of them."

"There are seven—"

"Any fucking box," he said quietly. "Any box. All of them, just one—any of them."

I walked over with all the boxes. He looked at two and then put the rest back down.

"Go to your room for a few minutes. Your mother and I are going to discuss this."

"There are values," my father said an hour later to begin the unprecedented second family meeting of the day, "that some people have—that many people have—that most people have. That we *understand*—that we *respect*, definitely—that are the prevailing values of the day, even, and we respect that, too, on its own terms, but. *But.* Respecting a value doesn't necessarily mean sharing that value—often, but not always—only sometimes, anyway. For your mother and I . . . We in this household . . . That's what we believe."

I had no idea what he was talking about. My mother looked

like she knew what he was supposed to be talking about, but not why he was saying it the way he was.

"We are not going to claim the prize," said my mother.

Now I understood why my father had answered in such a nonsensical way: what he was trying to say made no sense.

"Why?"

"Because it's based on actions that we don't allow in this household," my mother said. "It's the result of broken rules."

"But I already broke the rule, and you forgave me," I said.

"It doesn't work like that," said my mother.

"Why don't you punish me for that," I said, "something fair, like grounding me, and then I'll keep the hundred thousand dollars. You wouldn't fine me a hundred thousand dollars just for going to the store when I wasn't allowed to, right? You'd ground me, right? So just ground me. Okay?"

"But everything that would follow would be based on breaking that rule," said my father. "So any change in our lives—and there would be a great many—would be following from a corrupt core, from a foundation of values we didn't believe in. Do you understand?"

"This is a test, in a way," said my mother. "A test of fate."

"Yes, except there's no such thing as fate, there are only consequences of previous actions, and coincidences, which are the consequences of factors and decisions which are too many and too minute to be aware of—"

"Okay," said my mother. "Okay, stop. In any case, it's a test of our values."

"How about this," I offered. "You put all the money in a college fund for me. I'm not even allowed to touch it until I get to college. And then, it's only to pay for college."

I stared at them, daring them to turn down a prospect as joyless as this one. If I won a hundred thousand dollars and it all went into a college fund, would it still be the greatest single letdown of my life? Yes. I had no interest in college; I planned to be a professional wrestler. But at this point I just needed to find out if this free-falling disappointment even had a floor.

"No," said my mother.

"That would still be basing everything on something that isn't our value system," said my father. "In terms of college, if you work hard, there are still plenty of ways to earn scholarships or find alternative paths toward a good education without a lot of money."

"I thought you said all of higher education was corrupt and based only on money," I said.

My mother looked at my father.

"I said that in a heated moment, in the midst of a stressful tenure . . . No, there . . . there are definitely ways . . ."

I no longer understood my parents.

"Can I at least keep the sugar cereals?" I asked.

They looked at each other.

"Yes," said my mother.

"*All* of them?"

They smiled, relieved to have this conversation end on the word "yes."

"Yes," they said.

"Okay," I said.

It wasn't okay at all, and looking back, I think that question represented the birth—forced under high pressure at the age when a moment like this is bound to be born anyway—of my first pulse of truly sophisticated manipulation.

In that instant, it had suddenly come to me that if I were to ask that adorably missing-the-point question, I would appear to them like the fifth grader who would leave it at that, who would trust that his parents were always right, instead of the fifth grader who now knew, with certainty and for the first time, that his parents were wrong and that it was his destiny to use all the powers he had, including a calculated flash of the belovedly unpredictable kid logic of their only child, to set things right.

Tom Salzberg was a fifth grader who was old for our grade and acted it. We weren't exactly friends, but I considered us respectful acquaintances, and I had a sense he would know what to do with this information. I found him at his locker in the three minutes between homeroom and library and quickly told him everything.

"Mm-hmm," he said. As if this happening were one of many things like this he had to balance today. As if it had happened before. "Mm-hmm. Do you know where the ticket is?"

I told him as we walked into library that I was pretty sure I knew where it was in the house and that in any event I could find it. To show him how much I meant business I rushed through a recap of how I had hidden my motives behind the "can I keep the sugar cereal" story, which I thought would at least amuse him, but even this abridged version he seemed to find uninteresting, and by now he was sitting at the one library computer terminal that had internet, which I knew meant I was about to lose his attention for good. "If you can get it by Thursday," he said, eyes fixed on the computer monitor, "we have a half day then for teacher meetings. We'll be out at eleven-thirty. Battle Creek, Michigan, is an hour and a half away. That's where Kellogg's headquarters is." He tilted the screen toward me and revealed a picture of an immense, futuristic, fortress of a building—the last

wholesome fantasy of a middle-school boy. "Tell your parents
you have a soccer game after school and my parents are giving you a ride home after dinner. Tell them that we're having
pizza." I didn't play soccer or eat pizza, but I accepted this story
unedited, and so did my mother when I got home from school
that afternoon.

There was then, in our house, an unused staircase behind the
kitchen that my mother had long ago decided was too steep
to be safe. Instead, it had been repurposed as a mostly empty
diagonal closet where my parents kept things like tax returns
and unwrapped presents. It was closed off by an unlocked door
on both sides, and while I had glanced quickly inside a handful
of times over the years whenever one of the doors had somehow slightly opened, I had never actually personally opened the
door, for fear of accidentally ruining my own birthday or the
still-ambiguous-by-mutual-agreement myth of Santa Claus.

Separately, I had, two years earlier, toward the beginning of
third grade, realized in an epiphany over an inspiringly decadent
breakfast-for-dinner that midnight was not actually the middle
of the night: if the night was something that started at 8:00 p.m.
and ended at 7:00 a.m., as I knew it to be, then the middle of the
night was actually 1:30 a.m. My parents happily confirmed this
for me. Although my bedtimes had shifted in the years since, I
still believed with stubborn auto-loyalty that 1:30 remained the
official unofficial middle of the night.

That night, I stared at my clock until it hit 1:29. Then I took
a full minute to step out of bed, wearing both socks and slippers,
determined to take no chances, and shuffled out of my room on
the heels of my feet, rather than tiptoe, which I had noted long

ago was actually more squeaky than "tip-heel," my own invention as far as I knew.

I stepped out and opened the door that I had walked by thousands of times, and then for the first time I took one step after another down the staircase, until I was alone amid the clutter and mystery, unarmed except for a small emergency flashlight that cast a small square light into the cold diagonal corridor, where everything was more or less the color of manila.

On top of a video game I had asked for a long time ago was a dust-free white envelope. I picked it up. It wasn't even licked shut. Inside was the winning strip of cardboard from the Corn Flakes box. I put it in my pajama-pants pocket and returned the envelope to where it was. I slipped back up the stairs, tip-heel the whole way, closed the staircase door, put the cardboard code under my pillow, and waited for 7:30, never closing my eyes except to blink, constantly checking for the code with my hands to make sure it hadn't somehow evaporated.

The dictionary that had been used for the now-even-more-irrelevant contest rematch was still on my dresser. Out of an instinct I didn't have the word to describe yet—irony? panache?—I put the winning code in the middle of that dictionary, put the dictionary in my backpack, and took it to school.

At lunch, I found Tom Salzberg in the cafeteria and showed him the scrap of cardboard.

Tom stared at the numerical code and the YOU ARE A WINNER message right below it for a long time. He had been convinced the whole thing was real when he had only my word to go on; now, staring at the actual evidence, he seemed somehow less sure.

"50-50," he finally said.

"No," I said. I hadn't expected to pay him anything. "80-20," I said.

He squinted in consideration for a second, then made a face identical to the Robert De Niro face that had failed to win him placement in the class talent show, and shook my hand.

"I'll buy the bus tickets with my mom's credit card, and then I'm going to call us a taxi to take us to the Greyhound station."

I had never been in a taxi before but didn't feel like letting him know that.

"Shotgun," I said.

The Battle Creek, Michigan, headquarters of Kellogg's looks like a spaceship built to look like a pyramid that was then hastily converted into a public library during a period of intergalactic peace. It looks exactly as you would hope it would look. As fun as it is to try to describe, I still recommend you look it up. It's really something, and it will help you imagine how it felt to be a pair of eleven-year-old boys walking up to it, secretly carrying a secret code worth one hundred thousand dollars in a backpack.

We walked through the glass doors as if we had a business meeting ourselves, as men and women streamed in and out of the building around us, none of them questioning our right to be there. When we finally reached the all-glass reception desk inside, I realized I didn't know what to say.

Tom did.

"Prize Department, please," said Tom.

"I'm sorry, how can I help you two?" said the reassuringly plain-looking woman at the desk, a woman with brown hair and plastic glasses who looked like she could have been one of our friendlier teachers.

"Prize Department—Sweepstakes Prize Subdivision," said Tom with even more authority. "Also check under Giveaways—Secret Code Redemption."

"Do you have a name, or a person you're looking for?" she asked. I took the winning code out of my backpack and—holding it tight with two hands, not trusting even this palpably kind woman, our one friend here so far—held it for her to see, but not touch.

"Oh my. Congratulations! How exciting. Are you two brothers?"

"No way," said Tom. "Prize Department, please."

"It's my ticket," I said.

"What's your name?" the woman asked. I gave her a copy of my school ID.

She paused as she read the name and looked at me again.

"Let me just copy this, and you wait here."

We sat on the stiff leather couch for five minutes until an extremely tall, extremely confident, very handsome and athletic-looking man in a notably soft-looking suit walked up to us and smiled. "Congratulations. Which of you is the winner?" he asked, but he was staring at me the whole time.

"I am," I said.

"Congratulations," he said again, extending a hand. I stood up so I could shake his hand appropriately, and he shook it so hard it hurt. "Come to my office and let's discuss this."

Tom stood up, too.

"Just the contest winner," said the man.

Tom kept standing. "It's a trap," he blurted, his voice breaking, exactly as our books on puberty had warned us might happen but had never happened so far. "It's a trap!"

"It's not a trap," said the man.

"What department are you in?" asked Tom. "Can we see some ID?"

"I'm Executive Vice-Chairman of the Kellogg's corporation," said the man in the suit, "and I don't need to show ID here."

Tom sat down.

The man gestured toward the long hallway ahead of us—*after you*, the gesture said—and even though I didn't know where we were going, he let me lead the way, until we got to the elevator and he pressed the top button, and he took it from there.

The office was huge, and quiet. Windows looked out over all of Michigan, to Grand Rapids and beyond; there were so many windows, or more accurately so much window, that the room was very bright even with none of the lights on. Little toys were neatly lined up across his long windowsill—a tiny basketball, a tiny pistol, a tiny lemon—each of them sitting on top of a bronze label on a plaque. On the walls were about a half dozen framed, colorful drawings, each signed by many children, thanking him for their "super" and "great" and "super great" experiences on field trips.

"You have an unusual last name," the man said, and then said all five syllables of it correctly.

I said yes, I had never met anyone else with it, and it seemed that no one could ever spell or pronounce it. I was impressed he had gotten it right.

He asked more easy and straightforward questions: who my parents were and what they did, what town I was from, whether I had brothers or sisters. It was a great relief, in the midst of such an intimidating situation and environment, to be asked questions I could answer without even trying to think. I kept talking, letting each answer of mine go longer than the last, which led him to even more questions. How's school? Public, private? Easy, hard? Sports? Baseball, soccer? Tigers, Red Wings? Video games? Friends, best friends, bullies, girls? What do you want to be when you grow up? How do you get along with your parents? Do they often buy Kellogg's products?

Before long everything tumbled out: how my parents had strict policies against both sugar cereals and name-brand cereals, even the healthy ones; how I had felt drawn to the box in the store anyway; how I had, to my embarrassment now, cried when I lost, which I knew I was too old to do; that very weird follow-up contest that my father had set up for me with the dictionary and the expression he made that I didn't know how to describe; how I had gone back to the store by myself after school; the bizarre and nonsensical things my parents had said about why it was somehow against our values to redeem the prize; how strange it had felt to be sure for the first time that my parents were wrong, and how frustrated and confused and angry it had made me; the staircase, Tom, 80-20, how the taxi driver didn't want to let me sit in the front seat for some reason.

After I said everything, he stared at me for a second and paused.

"I can't give you the prize."

My mind first went to Tom, warning me that this was a trap.

"Regulations prohibit families of Kellogg's employees from participating in this contest or claiming a prize," he said. Then he smiled, and there was—the only time I've ever seen this in real life, and a phrase I had never been able to quite understand until now—a glint in this person's eyes.

"And I'm your father."

"I'm going to tell you a story. And then you tell me what you want to do.

"Twelve years ago, I was a visiting lecturer at the Steven M. Ross School of Business at the University of Michigan in Ann Arbor. I was twenty-nine years old at the time. I was the youngest Senior Vice President in the history of Kellogg's. I had called up the school myself and offered my services as a visiting lecturer for one semester. I explained how it was important to give something back to the community, be a role model, to whom much is given much is expected, all that. But that wasn't it at all. By the way, if I never see you again, and end up teaching nothing else to you—that's the one thing I want you to have learned from me. People—even good, impressive people—always want something simple and unimpressive. Everything good and impressive that they do in their lives is a result of the impressive path they take to get what they want—not a result of wanting an impressive thing. It's what brought me here. It's what brought you here.

"I was really giving myself one semester—that's only three months—to find a wife. Someone genuine and beautiful and interesting, and someone outside the circles in which I lived. This wasn't much time, but I was an overachiever, and confident, and I was used to accomplishing major things in very set periods of time.

"On the first day of the first class, I saw her. The reason I was there—I knew that right away. Pale, freckles, hair in a messy, frizzy light poof. T-shirt. Beautiful. Last seat of the last row. She looked like she didn't want to be there, and she didn't: it turned out she was a French literature major, and this class was the economics requirement that she had delayed until her final semester because she hated anything that had to do with money. So I wasn't in the best position to impress her. Which I liked, too.

"There were twenty students in the class, so I was able to

institute fifteen-minute meetings with each student individually each week. I scheduled hers last, on Friday afternoons. I was even more taken upon second sight than I was at first. She was brilliant and sarcastic; inner fire, light touch, certain of her values, which I had a sense were better than mine and which I wanted to learn from. I was sold.

"Now, there were two pretty considerable obstacles in my path. The woman was about to become engaged to the only man she had ever dated, her boyfriend of five years, a man she told me she loved definitively. And in addition to that, she went out of her way to make it clear that, separately, she had absolutely no attraction to or interest in me as a person. She emphasized these things a little gratuitously, in fact." He laughed.

"I continued to meet each of the students once a week for the twelve weeks of the class, just to justify seeing this woman. Every week when the two of us sat down, I started with the same question: 'How's your boyfriend?' 'Couldn't be better' was her answer every time, and then we would run out the rest of the fifteen minutes in a conversation about basic economics that neither of us had any interest in. This was nine weeks. The tenth week, I didn't ask my opening question, and we just talked about economics the whole time. The eleventh week, she brought up her boyfriend right away and walked me through her doubts about the relationship for the entirety of the session, which this time ran almost an hour.

"On the final week of the semester, she told me that she was questioning everything in her life, that her relationship had in fact been over for some time, and that she didn't know what to do. We continued to talk about this for the rest of the afternoon, over dinner that night, and the next morning over a balanced breakfast.

"She stopped returning my phone calls immediately and

moved out of her dormitory. After several weeks, I tracked down her parents' residence through a student directory to which I was not supposed to have access, and she picked up the phone in another room and delivered all the following news in the space of about a minute: she was pregnant, she was getting married within the month, and it had taken her brief time with me to make her realize that her boyfriend was and would always be the love of her life. I was never to contact her again. They were in love, she said.

"I was in love, too. I suggested that I might contact her fiancé and tell him everything, including my theories as to the timing of the pregnancy. She said she had already told him everything, that they were determined to raise the child as theirs, and that I was not welcome in their lives in any way. She raised the prospect of a restraining order against me and, more chillingly, whatever reputation-ruining accusations would be necessary for her to obtain one.

"But it was actually her passion that gave me pause, not her threats. Because while I knew I was in love, I could see that my love wasn't as big as their love, and I decided that was reason enough for me to retreat. That's the part that I've questioned since, and I'll tell you why in a moment.

"Now, as you can see"—he leaned back and gestured around the office and to the immense window behind him—"I have an excellent career and, all in all, an excellent life. But I was right to try to act fast in that three-month semester: in the dozen years since, I have not come close to finding a person I've wanted to share that life with. Not anywhere close. So I share my life with no one. I am happy—make no mistake. The life I live alone is a great one. But I do wish I had a family. It's the rare goal that has eluded me so far.

"Your parents love each other very much. From the information I know, I wouldn't try to argue that they are anything less than one of the great love stories of our age. That they would sacrifice everything—from money, to truth, to enjoyment of the universally acknowledged finest breakfast cereals in America— just to stay loyal to each other, and to the family they were determined to have together? It's something. It really is.

"But I ask you—and I can tell you're smart enough to grapple with a real question: is love such a strong force that it needs to be obeyed by the people who lie outside it?

"Think about this, specifically. The love of your mother for the man you know as your father is the ultimate force known to those experiencing it. Fair. Fine. But to anyone else? To me? To you? Is it selfish to impose the consequences of your love— infinite only to you—on the lives of others? If it means denying someone something as big as the life he was meant to have?"

He pointed to me with the same hand that had gestured out the window. "What sneakers do you wear? What musical instruments can you play? What languages do you speak? Have you ever been to the Olympics? Read a book in a café in Barcelona? Pretended to read a book in a café in Barcelona? What colleges does it not even occur to you to wonder about?"

I asked him if he thought, like my mother did, that this was a test of fate.

"It certainly feels like fate in this moment, doesn't it?" he said, smiling. "But if you really think about it, it's actually more magical, more special—more faithful, even, in the bigger way, and to say nothing of more true—to not believe in fate.

"Fate, to me, simply means that all the billions of microscopic actions we can't calculate lead to consequences that feel right because they *are* right. They fit, they follow. We can't see and understand all the causes behind everything, but I think it's more magical to accept that they're there than it is to believe that they're not, and that something called 'fate' is filling all that space instead.

"Whatever you call it, fate, not-fate—and I usually do just call this fate, by the way, just because it's simpler, it sounds more optimistic, more true to the spirit of what I mean—it's better branding—but whatever it was, something in your nature drew you to that cereal box in the store. The promise of bigger things, of brighter colors, better tastes. Curiosity. Chance. Fun. The promise of money. Hope. The feeling of being a part of the national experience—populism, you could call it; patriotism, you could call it. Then you were told that this cereal wasn't something you could have—and you broke a rule. You broke several rules, and you never break rules—that's how loud this called to you. I don't believe it was fate that did this, to speak honestly, no. I believe it was bigger than that. Grander than that. Because these are drives that are in your blood—just the way that they're in mine. If you were someone else's son, these drives wouldn't be in you, and you wouldn't have been drawn to that box the way you were. These drives are not, with all due respect, in the blood of a philosophy professor who would say that he doesn't believe in sugar cereals on principle. And I actually mean that phrase— 'with all due respect'—because I *do* respect it. It's just not me. And it's sure as hell not you. Because when you won the prize and then were told the prize wasn't something you could have, that didn't work for you. The exact same way it wouldn't have worked for me. Something in your nature was telling you that the rules of your childhood home weren't the rules of your life anymore. You broke those rules and then kept breaking them, because you wouldn't let anything stand between you and what you knew you were destined to have. You followed an impulse. A chain of impulses. Impulses that were there for a reason. And now, here you are.

"Your parents lied, too, remember. They wouldn't allow popular cereals into the house not because of the price or because they aren't healthy—I could give you a stack of nutritional information comparing our cereals with the homemade pancakes you told me you eat several times a week—but because of the personal associations for them. And they wouldn't let you claim your prize because they knew it would lead you to learn the truth. They knew that sweepstakes of this kind are never applicable for family members of company employees and that even the most perfunctory background check by the company, especially with a last name as distinct as yours—even Beverly, at the desk, whom I've known for twenty years, noticed it—would lead someone in some department to take notice and allow us— force us, by federal law—to not only deny you the prize, but also blow up this family mythology they already sacrificed so much in order to invent and protect. Look, I can't blame them. You're an extraordinary young person.

"So, as I've said, I can't offer you the prize. But I can offer you something else."

A part of me wondered if he was going to pull a dictionary down from the wall.

"You can be my son."

He handed me a business card.

"Think it over. Think about who you are and how you see yourself going forward. And if it makes sense to you, give me a call. Don't let your mother see this, of course."

He shook my hand again, just as hard.

Tom leapt up off the couch when he saw me cross back into the lobby.

"What happened? How did it go?"

"It's called the Promotions Department, idiot," I said. "Not the Prize Department."

On the bus ride back to Grand Rapids, I stared out the window for the hour and a half.

I imagined what Michigan would look like—or what it would feel like to look out at Michigan—if I were the kid of the executive, and then if I were just the kid of my family.

The two feelings felt very different.

I liked them both.

I liked the feeling of being able to switch back and forth in my mind, too.

I wished the bus ride were longer.

"How was Tom's? How was pizza?"

I forgot all about the lie I had told my mother, that I was having pizza at Tom's. It seemed quaint, and cozy, and sad.

"It was good."

"What kind did you get?"

"Pineapple."

"Yum! You have room for dessert?"

"Yes," I said. "Why?"

"What do you mean, 'why'?" my mother laughed. "In case you want to have dessert with us!" I looked over into the kitchen and saw my dad in his sweater, making a pot of mint tea the way he always did after dinner.

I loved my parents so much.

"Go upstairs and put your things away," said my mother. "It'll be ready in about five. Ice cream sundaes."

I went up to my room and took the business card out of my pocket. I noticed that it was now completely crumpled from how tightly I must have held it on the bus ride back.

I put the business card in the dictionary and came down for dessert.

My father set out three teacups and three ice-cream bowls.

"Would you like some tea?"

"Yes, please," I said. "Thank you."

"It'll go well with the ice cream," said my mother. "Hot and cold."

I noticed a tub of frozen yogurt on the table.

"Is there ice cream?"

"This is the ice cream," said my father about the yogurt. "You put whipped cream and sauce on this, and all buried in a sundae, you don't know the difference."

"Okay," I said.

"Except there's no whipped cream," said my mother.

"Then why did you say it?" I asked.

"Hypothetically," he said.

"Okay," I said. "Can you pass the chocolate sauce?"

He handed me a fragile-looking glass bottle.

"We don't have chocolate sauce. This is agave syrup."

"I met my real father today," I said.

It wasn't that I didn't love my parents after that. I did, and I still do. We're still in touch.

But while I loved my family, I also knew that it wasn't who I was anymore. If it ever even had been.

I was a name-brand kid, and I was meant to have a name-brand life.

Sometimes I wish I had learned everything earlier and that my real life could have started sooner. Other times, I'm glad that the first part of my life lasted as long as it did. It doesn't really matter, though. None of it could have been any different.

As for fate—or not-fate—I'm still not sure about it, but it's not something that keeps me up at night. I've lived it, and the people who still wonder about that kind of thing can call it whatever they want.

↶ The Man Who Posted Pictures of Everything He Ate

Once there was a man who posted pictures online of most of the things he ate. He put up pictures of most of his meals and some of his snacks with little captions.

> Yum!!
> I made this myself!
> Hits the spot.
> Saaaaalty!
> I'm gonna regret this tomorrow!!!
> Yum!!

And plenty of times—most of the time—he simply let the pictures speak for themselves.

The sixteen, then fifteen, then sixteen, then fourteen people who followed him made fun of him for it mercilessly.

> Why do you post pictures of your food?!
> We don't give a **** what u ate!!

The more they teased him, the more he did it, and the more he did it, the more they teased him.

why do u always post pics of ur food!?

He did it because it made him feel like he was eating his meals with more people.

It was the same reason he liked the teasing.

⌒⇀ Closure

"I want closure."

"There's no such thing as closure."

"Please. I have to see you. Please. Please."

"No."

"One last time."

"No."

"Real quick. Ten minutes. Five minutes. One minute."

"Annette, we have nothing to talk about. You know I love you. But I'm at this point—"

"I know, I know! I can't hear all this again! Please! I just need closure."

"There's no such thing as closure."

"I just need closure. I know I can get closure. Ten minutes. Please!"

"Okay. When?"

"Let's meet at the bench by the river. Right now. Where we had our first kiss."

"Now? The bench by ... At eleven at night? Come on, Annette. Can you ... can you just come over?"

"Come over?"

"I mean, just, it's late, and if it's so important for this to be *right now*—"

"That's not what this is about!"

"No, I didn't mean—"

"I need closure, David. I just need closure."

David met Annette by the river.

"Wow. You look really amazing."

"Thank you," said Annette with a two-blinks-and-you'd-miss-it half curtsey at once feminine and mean.

For the first time in her life, Annette looked exactly the way she wanted to look. Her hair was mostly neat, mostly down; she wore a simple dress that was the exact medium shade of red of all the shades of red in the world. It wasn't even that hard to look this way, she noted as she caught a last look at herself in the mirror on her way out; it just took some effort and thought and luck—a reasonable but attainable amount more of each than usual. A good lesson to learn for the future, she thought; a future that could begin tonight, right after she got closure.

"I want to say something."

"Okay."

"Everything is okay."

She smiled. He smiled back.

"Everything in the past," continued Annette, "is in the past. The cheating—the cheating you admit to, and the cheating you still can't bring yourself to admit to—"

"Wait, Annette—"

"And the lies *about* the cheating—the stories you made up that you eventually felt more loyal to than you did to the relationship—"

"Annette—"

"It's all okay! I'm saying it's all okay! All the times you made me feel like your backup choice when it would have been so simple to just tell me I looked beautiful; all the times you made me feel like the girl you were just killing time with while you waited to find your true love, even though you knew I loved you; or the times you made me feel like your stupid little sister, or your employee—"

"Annette—"

"No, I forgive all of it. You don't have to admit it or even accept it. I choose to let it go. I don't want to carry it around in my heart anymore."

"Okay . . . Well, Annette—"

He paused, then rushed to make up for whatever the pause had cost him.

"Annette, just because I'm accepting this doesn't mean I'm conceding anything you say is true—"

"You don't have to," she smiled. "It's all in the past. It's all over."

"Okay, well, that's good. Some of what you're saying is unnecessary and implies, I think, an excessive level of . . . I mean, I understand, as a thought exercise, for the sake of—"

"Now I want to kiss you."

"Annette . . ."

"A goodbye kiss. Just one. For closure."

Annette took a step toward him.

Closure, so close.

"Annette . . . I want to . . . But I don't think . . . God, you look beautiful, trust me, it's not . . . But this is, I'm kind of seeing someone, and—"

"One kiss! You don't even have to kiss back. I just need to kiss you goodbye. For closure. One last time. Okay?"

"Okay."

"Open your mouth and close your eyes," said Annette, coyly.

"I thought you said I didn't have to kiss back," said David, coyly.

"Well, then you can keep your mouth closed, if you want," said Annette, coyly.

David half opened his mouth and closed his eyes.

Annette kissed him.

While she held the kiss she pictured everything she could remember from the relationship, in chronological order, from the first email to the last text message, and every kiss and laugh and fight in between. When she had pictured absolutely everything she could bring herself to remember, which was everything, she visualized herself literally kissing the block letters of the word GOODBYE.

As the E started to fade in her mind, and her real lips stayed on his real mouth, she held out her left hand and snapped her thumb and index finger together—the softer and more difficult version of the snap—and eight men masked in black descended swiftly toward her ex-boyfriend, quiet enough for all their footsteps to be flattened by the squish of her kiss.

The first man injected David's neck with a clear liquid that knocked him unconscious. A second man pulled David's phone out of his front pocket, right where Annette had told him it would be. Two men wheeled out a cement box from behind a parked truck and removed two sacks of beach sand, and then a fifth masked man joined them to lift the unconscious body into the box, then split open the sacks of sand and fill the rest of the box to the top. A sixth man fastened a cement lid to the top of the box on a preset row of hinges and then, together with the third and fourth men, carried the box to the edge of the river and tilted it in, while the seventh man swept up all the miscellaneous bits of debris that had accumulated into an opaque plastic bag. The second man, still holding the phone of the man in the box, showed what he had been typing into the phone to the eighth masked man, who had been simply watching everything as it unfolded and nodding, and who now nodded more as he read:

To everyone I love (and a few who just got on this list off my spam folder, haha!): I'm writing because I needed you to know that after a lot of soul-searching I've decided I need to "drop out" for a while (as it were). A lot of you know that I was having a lot of anxiety about things, esp. with my most recent relationship(s), and I decided I need to kind of take some time off and really just *think* and *be myself* for a while with no distractions and no influence—just for a while!!—from the people who have made me, well … me. I'll be getting some much needed rest & solitude. Maybe I'll finally take that motorcycle trip across Central America that I'm always talking about—although I guess first I'll have to get a motorcycle license (and learn how to change a tire!). Ha. Also, my plan is to watch all five seasons of The Wire while I'm away, so when I am back, at least I'll finally have something to talk to you all about! Anyway, I love you all so, so much, and thank you for respecting this need of mine right now. And, again, do not worry about me just because I'm out of contact. This really is the best thing that could happen to me. Have fun, I love you all and miss you already. Love you and thanks for understanding this.

Sent from my Phone—forgiive tha typoooes&&1*&☺.

The eighth man showed the phone to Annette, who nodded, and then handed the phone back to the second man, who pressed a button that sent the email to every contact in the phone.

Then the second man plugged a new program into the phone. It was an application called Closure, and according to the people on the since-deleted message board who had recommended this team, it was what meant the difference between being the best at this and being only one of the best.

The program, using data that Annette had provided to them in advance, was said to be able to infiltrate every record-keeping website and database that had ever recorded the existence of her ex-boyfriend and erase all written and photographic evidence of him that was labeled by any of the four most common spellings of his full name. The program was guaranteed to work in under ten minutes. It finished in six and a half, and when it was done, the second man threw the phone into the river, where it, too, died instantly and anonymously.

That was it.

Annette approached the eighth man, pulled fifty one-hundred-dollar bills from her purse; handed them to him in a roll; and then impulsively kissed him on the side of the mask, making him blush, or so she imagined.

"Congratulations," said the eighth man. "The first person to truly achieve closure."

"Am I really the first?"

"Well, if you weren't, I guess I couldn't tell you, could I?"

The eight men walked away and got back in their surprisingly domestic-looking minivan and drove off, leaving Annette, heart racing, all alone.

There was a beaded line of sweat across her forehead, which she wiped off, and her lipstick was smeared a bit, which she corrected; now she looked close to perfect, which, she had always suspected, was actually a little hotter than perfect.

She walked alone to her favorite bar, ordered her favorite drink, and stirred it as she waited for the rest of her life to approach.

⌁ Kindness Among Cakes

CHILD: "Why does carrot cake have the best icing?"
MOTHER: "Because it needs the best icing."

Quantum Nonlocality and the Death of Elvis Presley

You may remember a time when the most common headline to see on a tabloid newspaper in the checkout aisle of the supermarket was that Elvis Presley had been seen alive. And you may remember that sometime around 1994, all these newspapers stopped saying that around the same time.

The papers had been making it all up. None of the pictures were real, and none of the details had anything to do with anything.

But they were right, too.

"People just can't accept the fact that the King is dead," one woman sighed to her son when he pointed to such a headline in a Kroger checkout aisle in 1986, back when children were confused by newspapers that contradicted other newspapers.

Behind them in line stood the dead king himself, holding Wonder Bread, peanut butter, Tylenol, and a magazine about something else entirely.

It had in fact been Elvis who couldn't accept that he was alive, who at a certain specific point could no longer understand on any level how this fat and tired man in Memphis, this man who combed his thinning hair and slept in his freckled skin, could possibly share the same name and memories as the most mythical creature that the world in his day had known.

It wasn't simply that he had gained weight, or gained years, or transformed in any natural human way that would have made sad but rational sense to anyone. It was something deeper inside, something that told him that, as strange as it sounded, there wasn't any true, unbroken line anymore directly connecting the man in whom he stood and Elvis.

Elvis.
Elvis!
ELVIS!

Who, really, could be Elvis?

He could trace it only as far back as a particular Monday morning when he poured himself a bowl of cereal as he did every day, turned on the television, sat down on his sofa, and then found himself suddenly overcome by a loud, hollow echo of a feeling—starting, somehow, in his ears—that told him that the old feeling had been gone for some time.

He spent the next few days waiting for this new feeling to fade away, but as the hours and moods came and went, the feeling didn't.

He wandered the hallways of his Elvis-themed home, squinting into the framed photographs on the walls. The black-and-white photographs looked like Elvis, but not like him. The color photographs looked like him, but not like Elvis.

He looked in the mirror, and the person he saw looked like him, and it looked like Elvis. But it didn't look like *he* was Elvis.

He wrote down his name on a pad of paper and stared at it: *ELVIS*. It looked like the Roman numerals for a made-up number, a number of a jumbled, indecipherable value, which was at least closer to how he felt than anything else so far.

It was strange to think that he wasn't Elvis anymore, but it was even stranger to think that he ever had been.

After a few months of worrying a lot and trying not to worry, Elvis started to wonder seriously if the feeling that he definitely was who he had once been would ever come back at all, except in out-of-focus flashes after a lot of pills.

It didn't make any sense, thought Elvis; but somehow, the line that makes someone the same person from day to day must have snapped inside him when he wasn't paying attention, which had been, he admitted to himself with a shameful shudder, a lot of the time. A knot had untied, a hinge had popped; he didn't know the exact intricacies of the mechanics of the soul, he was simply a singer—or Elvis was, anyway; or had been—but in any case, however it had happened, the man he was now had just kept on going, unaware and untethered to whatever had once made him Elvis, and by the time he had realized it and turned back around, the real Elvis had somehow left the building.

But Elvis wasn't going to give up something as big as being Elvis without a fight.

If Elvis wanted to feel like Elvis again, thought Elvis, he was going to act like Elvis.

Elvis came up with a plan.

He would set out on a live tour across America—the grandest of his age. He would wear a suit of sparkling jewels—something that only a king of rock and roll could wear. He would sing each and every one of Elvis's hits, one after another, while standing in front of a giant flashing sign that said ELVIS—just so there would be no mistaking, for him or anyone else, who he was.

He did it. And each night he felt like Elvis again, for a couple of hours.

But then the day after each show, he would feel worse than before. In the tender light of early afternoon he would realize all over again that the person onstage the night before was still not quite Elvis; except now, he would realize in a panic, the situation was far worse: now that all these thousands of people had seen this not-quite Elvis and had been told in no uncertain terms that this *was* Elvis, that meant this new, almost-Elvis was replacing and erasing—show by show, ten thousand by ten thousand—the Elvis that he did know, for sure, had once been real, and true, and not this.

He wanted to die. No, that wasn't it: he wanted to breathe and eat and remember, to laugh at funny movies and practice his karate. But the more he kept living his life trying to be this other person, the more he knew he was harming that person; and he loved that other person more than he loved himself; and he knew that wasn't crazy, because everyone else did, too.

He told the Colonel that it was time for Elvis to die. He wasn't as articulate as he should have been, given the sensitive nature of the request, but luckily, the Colonel understood. The Colonel always did. "I'll take care of it," said Colonel Tom Parker, and on August 16, 1977, the body of Elvis Presley was found dead in Graceland.

Elvis woke up in Las Vegas. For a while he couldn't tell if he was in heaven or hell, but when he realized he was in Las Vegas, he knew he'd be okay.

Now that the king was dead, the man could do as he wished.

Elvis wondered what a regular person who wasn't Elvis would do now, and he reasoned that person would get a job. He looked around for something that paid well enough for work he would be able to do.

Before long, he found such a job, and became an Elvis impersonator.

Once again, he was the best in the world at something he loved.

"You're incredible!" people would tell him after his shows. "Incredible!"

"Thank you, thank you very much."

Afterward, when he walked down the street, people would wave at him: happily, affectionately. And, most exciting of all: casually.

"Hey, it's Elvis!"

He would wave back, the same way, and they'd both smile and forget about the moment a moment later.

He was finally who he had long wanted to be: a person for whom Elvis Presley was a major part of his life, but not everything.

And then there was the undeniable and all-American pleasure of being well paid for a job he found easy.

It wasn't the best time of his life; he had, after all, once been

Elvis—*Elvis!*—but it wasn't the worst time of his life anymore, either.

It was a time of his life.

Elvis died the second time in 1994, this time of a heart attack in the early morning hours at the breakfast counter of a diner on South Las Vegas Boulevard. A waitress found him over a grilled-cheese sandwich with an untouched half a grapefruit to its side. The only identification he had on him said *Elvis Aaron Presley* with the birth date *1/8/35* and the address of Graceland in Memphis, Tennessee.

This was something that happened from time to time in Las Vegas.

The second time, Elvis died happy.

And that was the moment—almost to the hour—that the tabloids stopped making up stories that Elvis had been seen here or there, and started making up things about people everyone already knew were alive, a tradition that continues to this day.

Maybe it was just a coincidence.

Or maybe when something that big is out there, a presence that size, it just doesn't go undetected. It has to be sensed, and said, by someone, in some way.

⌒↝ If I Had a Nickel

If I had a nickel for every time I spilled a cup of coffee, I'd be rich!

Here's how I'd do it.

1. SETUP AND EXPENSES

First: the coffee. At Costco you can get a 12-pack of 34-ounce cans of Folgers coffee for $65.99. Each of those makes 270 cups, which comes out to 2.04 cents a cup. An industrial-strength filter-free coffee brewer capable of brewing 40 cups at a time costs $119.99 at Costco. Five of these will be a one-time expense of $599.95. Costco also sells a 1,000-count box of 12-ounce paper cups for $116, which comes out to 11.6 cents a cup and to 1.16 cents per use of cup (based on a conservative estimate of ten spills per cup). I do not have a Costco card, but I can borrow one from a friend.

In terms of a workspace, a 1500 square foot space downtown with easy-to-wipe floors rents for $750 per month. While this is technically the kind of work one could do at home, I believe in keeping work and home life separate when possible for psychological reasons, especially in an enterprise such as this one, which I can easily envision driving a person insane. Mental health is an issue I take very seriously.

The single biggest one-time expense that I anticipate would be the construction and installation of a waist-high circuitous conveyor belt that would deliver cups of coffee from one side of the room to the other at a speed of four miles per hour, allowing proper time for me to retrieve and spill coffee cups on one end of the room while an assistant restocks and refills the coffee cups at the other end of the conveyor belt. I would estimate $14,400 for construction and installation (this is a ballpark estimate because none of the custom-conveyor companies I consulted understood the nature of the request) which can be amortized over the length of the enterprise.

2. STAFF

I would require one full-time assistant dedicated to preparing the next batch of coffee while I am busy spilling the current one and one additional full-time assistant simultaneously dedicated to cleaning the debris of the previous group of spills while I am on to the next. This system of cleanliness and order will help provide a situation of maximum safety, sanitation, and efficiency, as well as maintaining the all-important positive psychological environment. (Once again, mental health is an issue of paramount importance to me.)

Alternatively, I could conceivably enlist two unpaid interns who would receive college credit instead of monetary payment, but then I'd have to spend time writing their evaluations: time I *could have* spent spilling coffee.

I am presuming minimum wage (and would in fact become very angry if one of these employees asked for more than minimum wage for this job, likely out of proportion, especially given the stressful work enviroment I anticipate for this enterprise). Staffing would come to a total of $116 per day.

3. MISCELLANEOUS & UNANTICIPATED COSTS

Rubber pants and other similar miscellaneous expenses too numerous and minor to list in full detail here should add up to no more than $1000 per year.

Cleaning materials when purchased in bulk from Costco should average no more than $50 per day.

Theft of company materials is likely to run as high as $1000 per year. (While I believe in paying minimum wage, I don't expect my workers to like me for it.)

Psychological counseling to handle the effects of devoting my life's work to this crushingly bizarre and isolating activity of no relevant value or connection to the wider world should run me approximately $750 per week.

4. NET INCOME

Finally, the fun part: time to knock these babies down and watch the nickels come pouring in!

Assuming that at full operational capacity with a functional 4-mph conveyor belt that averages one spill of coffee per two seconds over the course of an eight-hour workday, we're looking at approximately 1800 spills per hour and 14,400 spills per workday.

At 5 cents per spilled cup of coffee, that comes to $720 per day, or $3600 per week, or $180,000 per year, allowing for two weeks of vacation per year, during which I envision myself going somewhere calm and cold.

5. TOTAL PROFITS

The total cost per spill associated with this process comes to 2.9 cents per cup, or $417.60 per day, or $104,400 per year. The remaining expenses total $52,232.00 annually.

These figures combined, and then subtracted from the previously calculated $180,000 net income from spilling approximately 3,600,000 cups of coffee per year at a compensation of five cents per spill, leave me with a total profit of $23,368 per year, before taxes.

6. CONCLUSION

So, maybe I wouldn't be rich, but I'd get by.

⌐⇀ A Good Problem to Have

When we were in the fourth grade, an old man burst into our classroom one day waving his rumpled little plaid arms and screaming. It might have been adorable if we had been old enough to find older people adorable, and also if it hadn't been a little bit scary.

"Stop! Is he saying anything about trains?! About train times?! Stop!"

Our teacher, Mr. Hunt, had a mustache and an inner calmness about him, and we never noticed that then he must have only been in his twenties. He put his arm lightly across the old man's back and led him to a big wooden chair in the corner of our class, a chair that none of us ever actually sat in but that might look to a visitor like a seat of honor.

"How can we help you?" asked Mr. Hunt.

"Are you asking them questions about trains?" asked the old man.

"No," said Mr. Hunt. "We're talking about geometry today. Can I help you with something? Would you like a glass of water?"

Mr. Hunt had an accent that my parents identified as a working-class one from Dorchester, Massachusetts. Some of us thought it made him sound cool, and some of us thought it made him sound like an old lady. Either one may have been why the old man seemed to calm down a little bit whenever Mr. Hunt spoke.

"Did he ever," exhaled the old man, who now rotated toward the class from the chair as if he were an amateur actor with stage fright in a community musical who was nonetheless following through on the play's plan to break the fourth wall, "ask you about trains? About trains leaving stations at different times?"

"Yes, I have," said Mr. Hunt.

"What textbook did you use? *Problems and Solutions Four*?"

"I got it from the internet."

A few of us gasped and then realized that Mr. Hunt didn't seem embarrassed about this, and then realized that we, too, got a lot of good stuff from the internet. Why shouldn't Mr. Hunt?

"The internet!" wailed the old man, his head sinking into his little hand. "No no no no no."

We all just watched him breathe for a second, like we had with the turtle our class had adopted earlier that year.

"Can I talk to you privately?" the man asked Mr. Hunt.

"Anything you have to say to me, you can say in front of my students," said Mr. Hunt. "Within the parameters of acceptable language."

"That's my problem," said the man.

He stared at us all at once, somehow, with a look that said that we knew what he was talking about, but we didn't.

"A man leaves Chicago at twelve p.m. on a train heading for Cleveland at sixty miles per hour," he said quickly. "Another man leaves Cleveland at one p.m. heading for Chicago on a train going eighty-five miles per hour. At what time will the two trains cross paths?"

One kid, Arush, raised his hand. "Approximately—"

"*I know the goddamn answer!*"

"*Language,*" said Mr. Hunt.

"And there's no 'approximately' in math," said the old man. "It's math. The answers are exact."

"The answers are exact," echoed Mr. Hunt, somewhat faintly. "Put your hand down, Arush."

"That's my problem," said the old man, sitting back down in the chair. "I wrote it. That was the one thing I did. The one thing. When you're young, you think everything you do is just the beginning. But when you're old, no matter who you are, you realize you only did one or two things."

We were silent. We had never heard anything like this before.

Some of us wondered what the one or two things we would do would be.

The old man smiled like it was over, but it wasn't.

"What I *did* not, *could* not, expect and *should never have* expected was that it would become the most famous math problem in the goddamn United States!"

"*Language.*"

"Pardon . . . Fine. What I did not expect was that every textbook in America would rip it off from the one I worked for and that I would end up taking home thirty-five dollars, yes, that's right, kids, a whopping *thirty-five dollars* for what would become the most famous math problem in America. Does that sound fair to you? What does that work out to per year?"

Arush raised his hand and Mr. Hunt signaled him to put it down.

"Mister?"

I spoke with what I believed was the right balance of politeness and confidence to get the old man's attention. "Sir? We actually learned the problem a little differently. Does that possibly make it different, in your opinion?"

The old man listened.

"We weren't asked where the trains would meet. We were just asked which would get to its destination faster."

"And," Mr. Hunt chimed in, "I taught it to them with Boston and New York."

"Everybody changes it," said the old man. "But when I came in here yelling about how they stole my problem, you all knew which problem I was yelling about, didn't you?"

We did.

"So that says a lot, doesn't it? If after all these years, you can recognize the basic spirit of something?"

It did.

"Would you care to tell us how you came up with it?" asked Mr. Hunt.

The man settled back into the big chair, and we could see how small he really was.

"Spring 1952," he said. "I was deployed in Europe, this is postwar—I was in the war, too, but I was sent back as part of a rebuilding effort in Belgium. I was homesick, more than during the war. I'm not afraid to admit that. I wasn't homesick during the war. I got married in between, to my wife."

He said the next part differently, and he looked out the window as he did: "*June.*

"I went again to earn extra money so we could build a family. I had my textbook job, and I could do that from anywhere, so this was like having two jobs. I was there ten months and one week before I was able to go home. I flew from Antwerp to London to New York—Idlewild, it was called then, the airport, before JFK died, before there was a JFK, well before JFK was JFK, anyway—and then to Chicago.

"Our home was in Columbus, Ohio. When I landed I phoned her from the airport and told her that I was taking the train right away from Chicago to Columbus, and it was only five hours away, she . . . *June*.

"She said she couldn't wait that long, now that I was so close. Can you believe that? Five more hours, after ten months, and she said she couldn't wait! She said she was going to hop on a train going toward me, too, and we would just have to meet in the middle. I said, June, that's crazy! But she insisted. And the real crazy thing is, secretly, I had been thinking the same thing.

"You have to understand what it was to be separated from someone back then. You're across an ocean; the world was just at war; now the Russians say they're going to bury us with a shoe. There are no rules anymore. And there's no telephone in your pants. You don't get news very often, and when you do, your heart pounds because it might be bad news. After all that, we couldn't take not being in sight of one another for a second more than we needed to.

"I did the math, and I kept doing it again and again on the train, how many minutes it would take to meet each other, estimating her train and my train at all these different speeds . . . Just looking at it every which way on the back of the train stationery envelope. They had stationery on trains back then—can you believe that? Everything was better then. Not everything," he said, looking at Arush, "but so much. So many things. Anyway. I don't know how I ever thought of it because I was only thinking about June, but I think your brain gets bigger at times like that because there was another part of my brain that thought, Boy, this would make one hell of a textbook problem.

"We met on the platform of the train station in Spencer, Ohio, exactly three hours and one minute after I got on the train, and we kissed for eleven minutes. They were the best eleven minutes of my life."

The girls and even a couple of the boys in the class applauded. The best-looking boy in the class, Tyler, made eye contact with Amanda, the best-looking girl in the class, and they both mouthed *Awwww* together, as though the two of them together had somehow had something to do with this.

Maybe Amanda wasn't the best-looking girl in the class. Maybe she was just the blondest.

"Wasn't it two guys in the textbook?" said one of four kids in our class named Matt. "Not, like, a guy and a girl?"

"I changed that part. I thought if it was a man and a woman, kids would get distracted and not focus on the math. Two men was a simpler thing back then. And anyway," said the man, "haven't you ever heard of artistic license? The point is, it's *my* life and *my* story. And it's my problem."

"It truly is a beautiful problem," said Mr. Hunt. "I mean, the math problem—not your problem. Your problem, we all hope you resolve it and get what you deserve."

"Thank you."

"But just in case," said Mr. Hunt, "look around at this classroom. Look. Generations of children have learned math from what you did, generations are a little bit smarter because of what you wrote. Doesn't that count for something?"

"It's nice," said the old man. "But shouldn't I be paid for it? If people are well paid for reality television and cotton candy and dunking a basketball, why can't they be well paid for changing young minds? I mean, wouldn't more people do it? Bright, selfish people? Nothing wrong with being selfish. If more people thought they could make a fortune curing cancer, wouldn't more people be trying to do that?" He turned to Mr. Hunt. "You, I don't need to explain this to you. You're a teacher."

Mr. Hunt smiled, a private type of smile that we all could see.

The old man made a lot of sense, except for the cotton candy reference. What was that about? Could you really make a lot of money that way? Maybe he knew someone who made a lot of money in candy. Or maybe he was just old, and you just had to ignore a few of the things he said to get to the wisdom.

I had an idea and raised my hand. I knew my idea was so good I didn't even wait to be called on.

Bright Ben, they sometimes called me in name games at the beginnings of school years.

Maybe it had affected me.

"Do you still have it?"

"Have what?"

"The train stationery."

"Maybe somewhere," said the man. "Why?"

"You could use it to prove you came up with the problem," I said. "Plus, you could even maybe sell the original to a museum."

Mr. Hunt murmured something to himself that sure sounded to me like "Bright Ben."

The old man coughed to clear his throat, even though it didn't sound like there was anything to clear. "Yes, it's in a shoebox. Or I think it is. I definitely know which one it would be in, anyway."

He acted like there wasn't anything more to say about this, even though there obviously was, so I spoke again, this time without raising my hand.

"Could you check?"

"Maybe," he said. "Maybe I could. That's the box where I put ... Where I put ... Letters, you know. That's where I put . . ." There were now longer and longer pauses between each word. "Pictures . . . that's . . ." Then that change in voice again: "*June.*"

Then just breathing for a while.

"You know, I did go through the box once. And it wasn't there. But I didn't look very carefully, though. I didn't even really look at all. Just put my hand in there and took it out. That's not really looking." He paused again. "But I'm not looking again. But maybe it's there. You know, maybe I'll look again. That's not a bad idea." But he said all of this like he knew he never would.

"Where do you live?" asked Mr. Hunt, gently. "Are you going to need any help getting back?"

"I live in Columbus. I told you that. I have my whole life. I figured I'd start out on the East Coast and then work my way back across the country. See with my own eyes just how big this problem is. Your class is my first stop, actually."

"You came here straight from Columbus, Ohio?"

"Yes."

"All the way to Massachusetts? All by yourself?"

"Yes."

"That's pretty far," said Mr. Hunt with concern. "How long did it take?"

"Nice try, nice try," said the old man. "You want your class to know how long my train took, you gotta pony up."

Everybody laughed at once, and the laughter seemed to surprise, and then lift, the old man.

"It is . . . I guess what you said before, it is nice seeing that you all know it," said the old man. "It's a reward. Not the only reward, but . . . you take what you can get. I'll try to get more, but you take what you can get. It's done so much good for the world that I do feel like I deserve more. But, yeah, that's a good thing."

"It's a good problem to have," said Mr. Hunt.

"Huh? What?" said the old man.

"I guess," said Mr. Hunt, louder and slower, "that in a way, it's a good problem to have."

"Oh. Ha," said the old man.

He walked to the door and put his hand on the doorknob, and we all waited for him to turn it, but he left it there for a very long time.

It's very suspenseful for someone to put a hand on a doorknob but not turn it, especially if he's old.

"*June* . . . the shoebox . . . good problem to have, too."

He opened the door and left.

"What the hell does that mean?" said one of the other Matts.

"*Language,*" said Mr. Hunt.

⌒→ Johnny Depp, Fate, and the Double-Decker Hollywood Tour Bus

The universe will tell you what it wants from you, if you listen to it. And one hot Friday in July, the universe told Johnny Depp what it wanted from him—not what it needed from him, because it definitely didn't need this—but what it wanted.

The sign came in the form of a red double-decker tour bus slowly rounding Mulholland Drive, the winding desert highway that tops the hills of Los Angeles and divides the sporadically glamorous city from the negligibly glamorous valley. Both sides glitter, and the tourists were dazzled by all of it, and Johnny Depp, riding alongside the bus, knew that if he took off his helmet, someone would notice him, and before long, it would be a big deal.

He was right: it was a very big deal. "JOHNNY DEPP!" The bus sped up slightly to match the pace of Johnny Depp, who kept fully focused on the road ahead as cameras flashed and bus riders waved. He was enough of a performer to know that playing it cool like this now would excite them more, in the long run, than if he waved back right away.

When he finally did wave, with a tiny *"who, me?"* that he saw Sean Penn use once in *Mystic River* and always envied, the bus went crazy.

Johnny Depp revved the engine and did a wheelie. The crowd broke into wild applause.

Before today, some of the more naive riders on the bus had bought into the notion that celebrity sightings were a regular feature of Los Angeles life, that a substantial proportion of the people in L.A. were the ones they had already heard of, and so while the sighting of Johnny Depp on a motorcycle had certainly delighted them, it had not shocked them. But this, now, was undeniably special, to everyone. Johnny Depp was showing off for them, doing tricks, and it really was something else.

In their excitement, both the bus and Johnny Depp had gradually sped up without noticing, and now Johnny Depp saw the heat-and-haze-weakened bites of light racing more and more quickly toward his motorcycle, and in an instant he realized that what was also approaching, in tandem, was an offer from the universe: legend or star, either one was fine, but he didn't have much time to decide, because the main way you recognize moments like these is by how fast they seem to be racing away.

Everyone dies, thought Johnny Depp as he raised both hands off the motorcycle, and flew into the drab valley below under a blanket of phone flashes and the eyes of newly born secondhand-legends; but not everyone is remembered like this.

Discussion question:

Do you think Johnny Depp should have driven his motorcycle off the mountain highway to his death? Why or why not?

⌒→ Being Young Was Her Thing

Being young was her thing, and she was the best at it. But every year, more and more girls came out of nowhere and tried to steal her thing.

One of these days I'm going to have to get a new thing, she thought to herself—but as quietly as she could, because she knew that if anyone ever caught her thinking this thought, her thing would be over right then.

Angel Echeverria, Comediante Superpopular

You only needed one great bit, and that was all he had. But that was all you needed.

He would do crowd work for twenty minutes, loosening the crowd up, throwing in some local references to life in the Bay Area and to Mexican American life at the turn of the millennium—basically just putting everyone at ease and letting them know he was one of them, which he was, and that he wasn't going to hassle anybody, which he wasn't.

Then he'd start the bit.

"You ever go into this store, Whole Foods, man? Everything is so expensive."

People were already laughing without even noticing that they were. Yes, of course they had been inside a Whole Foods, and yes, of course they had noticed the higher prices.

"But you know why it's so expensive? It's all up to the food. It's all in the food's mind. It's because of how the food *thinks* of itself." He pointed to his brain. "The food *believes* in itself, man. It has *confidence*. It has self-respect. It has self-*worth*. You just have to look at the labels: SOY NUTS."

He held his expression and waited for the quickest pockets

of the crowd to catch on and spread the laughter to the people around them. It usually took between five and five and a half seconds to reach its peak.

"soy *milk.*" Now the whole crowd was with him.

"The food knows what it is, man! It *proclaims* it!"

He was killing, and there was no looking back now.

"You go into Albertsons or Vons or, you know, that knockoff Vons, Jons?" Yes, they knew. "You see the shelves?" He went into his shopper voice (which was also his cop voice): "What's this? Who are you?" Now he shrugged his body deep into his shoulders and adopted the voice of a wimpy, moody adolescent boy: "Miiiiilk."

This was it, this was the bit all right—the one they had paid to see without even knowing what it would be—and he wasn't going to let it go anytime soon.

"Who are you?" repeated the cop/shopper. "Nuts, I *guess,*" said the same dumb, shy boy through Angel Echeverria's microphone, shyly shuffling his feet, one on top of the other. "I *guess* I'm nuts. I don't know if you want to buy me.'" Angel Echeverria then reclaimed his confident self again, a confidence lifted subtly but perceptibly higher than before by the knowledge coursing through his body that he now was so thoroughly destroying the audience he so loved. "You go into Whole Foods? *SOY NUTS!!!*" He pounded his fist proudly on an invisible podium and waited—not even for the sake of timing now, but for people to pause and literally replenish their breath so they would be physically able to laugh more. "*YO* SOY *SAUCE! CÓMPRAME!*" He could now slip in and out of English and Spanish and they wouldn't even notice the transition; it was as if he weren't a comedian anymore but the voice in their own heads entertaining them at this point. "*Sí, yo tengo una identidad, un* confidence, *un* pride. *YO SE QUIÉN YO SOY!* I am *worth* it!" He strutted around the stage, elbows high, being for the crowd a proud bottle of soy sauce with a smile headed skyward as the men and women in the audience, enveloped in the comfort of being entertained and the elation of being understood, applauded and cheered as long as they could, minutes on end, to express a gratitude that would last for months.

Everyone who saw Angel Echeverria saw him a second time, but no one saw him a third. They all wished he would find a new bit as good as the Whole Foods bit, and so did he. But he had what he had and he did what he did, and everyone remembered him fondly.

☞ The Market Was Down

Nobody knew why the market was down that day. But it didn't stop everyone from having a theory.

"Worries over Spain's role in the EU brought the market down today," said a woman on the radio. "The market had an off day today, due to uncertainty in oil futures," announced a man on television. "Market Slightly Down as Health Care Details Come into Focus" wrote a newspaper writer.

The truth was no one knew why the market was down. It started the day, just . . . down. It stayed down most of the day. It had an up moment for a little bit around lunch, but was still, just, down.

Why was the market down? No reason. Well, stupid stuff. Actually, to be honest, maybe it was Spain at the beginning, but it was really only worried about Spain because it woke up looking for something to worry about. Then, before long, the market started worrying about bigger things, things that didn't seem to have an answer.

If the market had never existed, would anyone miss it? Would anything really be different? Did anyone actually really care about the market, or did they just think they could make money from it? And then there were all those people who said they hated the market, and they always seemed so much cooler and better looking than the people who liked the market—were those people right? Were they on to something? Was the market soulless? Evil? Pointless? Harmful? Bad?

The market calmed down for a minute when it pictured Warren Buffett. What an undeniably warm, wise, lovely man Warren Buffett was! And he sure loved the market. With all his heart, without question. That made the market feel better.

But then the market thought of something so sad it made it want to kill itself: what if Warren Buffett was just wrong? This made the market feel worse than ever: the idea that an obviously wonderful old man like Warren Buffett might have wasted his heart loving something as terrible and worthless as itself, the market. Now the market felt so guilty and terrible it let itself wonder what it would be like if it let itself completely collapse. But it didn't. Oh, that's ridiculous, the market told itself: now you're just down because you're down. Come on. Look alive.

The market began to pick itself up a bit. People were happy to see the market improve—everyone was rooting for it (except for a few people who were always betting on the market to fail, but there would always be people like that; and those were people that even the people who hated the market hated). When the market realized how many people were counting on it, and how many people were hoping it got better, that made it pick itself up a little more. It felt more valued, more confident. Feeling that way made it look that way, too, and that made more people treat it that way. And that made it feel that way even more.

It was still down, though. Just kind of down.

What time was it? It felt late.

The thing was, the market could only be what it was. That's what it was: the market. Some people would always love it; some people would always hate it. Was it good? Was it bad? It wasn't its job to know. It was just its job to be what it was.

As the sun started to burn its way down in the sky, the market decided to just stop thinking for a while, stop working for a while, and get some rest.

The next day, the market was up!

⌒ The Vague Restaurant Critic

"More satisfying than a candy bar, but less satisfying than love," wrote the vague restaurant critic in his debut review.

"This is not helpful at all," murmured his readers to themselves, meaning no harm as they went elsewhere to find information more like what they had been looking for.

Before the vague restaurant critic could write a second review, he was fired.

A couple of weeks more and he might have caught on. He might have developed a following beyond the world of the traditional restaurant review readers for what he was doing, for the statement he was trying to make—about criticism, about restaurants, about our expectations in life on a larger level.

But he was fired before any of that could happen.

If it was even going to happen.

He didn't care. He knew what he did.

But he kind of did care. He wished other people knew what he did, too.

One of These Days, We Have to Do Something About Willie

We had all known for years that someday, sooner or later, we would have to do something about Willie.

We knew this from the night we met him: freshman year, orientation week, at the first real party we went to—the first party that didn't have ice cream. He was standing by the speakers, spinning pop-rap songs off the click-wheel edition of the iPod; he looked untroubled beyond his years, a life-sized version of the people you see on trophies; he seemed to be blazing outside the lines of his own body, as if he were drawn in crayon by an excited five-year-old; whatever fuel source was powering him couldn't possibly be sustainable, and its excess poured easily off of him in the form of expansive declarations about how awesome the party was, an enthusiasm that somehow circled back in order to power, even overpower, the party that was powering him; and when he noticed the three of us, all aspirants to social normalcy who had chosen this college partly because it scored higher than average among schools of its academic caliber under the "Party School" index on the *U.S. News & World Report* college guide, he decided in that moment, for some reason we would never understand or question, that he loved us, and that we would forever be at the center of his infinitely expanding galaxy of friends.

I think we knew even then how much he was going to transform our lives; and that eventually, to pay him back, we really would have to do something about him.

After college, the four of us all moved to different cities. I moved to New York to work as a copy editor for an alternative weekly (not the one you're thinking of); Josh went to San Francisco to work for a video-sharing website (not the one you're thinking of); Dave spent three months of an intended year backpacking alone through Japan and Singapore and then hastily abandoned it to go home to Chicago and apply to law school; and Willie, with more than enough alum connections to make up for a general studies diploma, got a job as an entry-level investment banker in Houston.

Even though we lived in different places, we still saw ourselves as moving through life as a group. It would have been great to get to see each other more—that was, in fact, one of our most frequent topics of conversation—but for four people pursuing their dreams in different cities, our presence in each other's lives really was quite substantial. We were more in touch with one another than with anyone else, including (if not especially) our families, and we gave one another as much advice and support as we ever had—more, even, because there was more to talk about, more decisions to make. We all still considered each other the closest people in each other's lives.

As that first year went on, though, the posts coming to us from Willie's corner of the internet became something that I felt more and more uncomfortable ignoring. By the January after graduation, almost every update from Willie's life involved a picture of him getting comedically (or was it dramatically?) incapacitated the night before, with captions to help tell the story even more clearly—"*TYPICAL MONDAY*," "*TYPICAL TUESDAY*," etc. A new photo of Willie passed out on a floor or out of control in a bar came across our screens literally every day. All these posts got nothing but favorable and favoriting comments and replies, except for one sensitive-looking girl named AliBaby90 who once asked "*r u okay?*" below a photo of Willie passed out, facedown, on a suburban lawn, to which Willie responded "*HAHA DO I LOOK OKAY?!!?*" which was apparently enough for her, since she "liked" the response.

Were we, in fact, really still friends—like we said we were, and thought we were, and which comforted us as we each staked out new lives in cities where we didn't really know anyone at all? Or, I wondered, were we just slowly transforming into simpler and more easily digestible fictional characters to one another—in other words, becoming our profile pictures: cool, expressionless Dave, unfazed even at majestic Mount Fuji, his much-remarked-upon good looks defiantly hidden behind sunglasses; sweetheart Josh, playfully presenting a prom corsage in a cookbook-filled suburban kitchen to his overjoyed six-year-old sister, standing on a table, playing along; me, as a preposterously anti-Semitic cartoon depiction of Woody Allen at a typewriter, drawn of me at the insistence of my girlfriend, Sarah, by a caricature artist in Times Square who knew only that I wanted to be a writer and that I looked, apparently, extremely Jewish; and Willie, drinking simultaneously from a handle of vodka and a handle of Jack Daniel's beneath a U-Haul at a tailgate party, surrounded by friends that didn't include us, screaming at someone or something, the photo filtered to look like an image that belonged in any era.

Except, I thought one day as I looked at that picture, wondering what my relationship to it was supposed to be—we didn't live in any era. We lived in the era when people treated things like alcoholism and addiction as the problems that they were, something that friends were supposed to save each other from.

Or something.

I tested out my doubts on the others when I would see their names online.

> Hey. Kind of worried about Willie?
> Seriously!! How hilarious is that guy.
> Yeah. I'm actually worried, though.
> Yeah, me too.

Everyone agreed that Willie seemed to have wandered into some territory where "out of control" and "out of control!!!" both got by security with the same ID. But he seemed to be self-aware about this—we always learned about his embarrassments directly from him, after all—and we didn't know what it was we would do about him, exactly, anyway. So it just became the same idea as always, but now sometimes with stars around it in our chats for emphasis—that one of these days, we were *really* going to have to do something about Willie.

Another few weeks went by, and then one day, Willie posted a photo of himself passed out next to a toilet with the caption: *"ROCK BOTTOM!!!"*

I called up everyone on the phone—another thing we had not done since college—and said we really had no excuse not to do something. Everyone agreed and then asked what I had in mind.

———

I had no idea what I had in mind. It felt like no one had ever been our age before.

I knew, in very general terms, from the references made on the television shows I did watch to the shows I didn't, and from the stray strands of D.A.R.E. that I hadn't wiped from my memory out of spite, that what we were supposed to do was stage some sort of formal intervention. It would have to be adapted a bit, made a little more personal and casual so that it would be able to fit our group of friends. But all interventions had some personal angle, probably? They were like weddings that way, probably, I figured? Take the traditional structure and make it just a little bit your own? That sounded right?

So, then, basically just a regular intervention?

First, we had to choose a place where we could all physically be together. One option was for us to all travel to Houston and ambush him there, but that had its drawbacks. I knew Willie lived alone in a high-rise apartment and kept "crazy" hours, so we wouldn't know how to get into his building or when he might be home. Plus, none of us really wanted to go to Houston.

I decided I would try to get him to come to us, so I had to come up with an event that would actually get him on a plane.

I knew from Facebook that Dave's birthday was coming up, so I announced a surprise birthday party for him in a month's time in Chicago. Willie responded *sounds like so much fun!!* and *would so love to be there!!!* and *will definitely try to make it!!!!* but that he had a *crazy-shifting work schedule* and *wouldn't know till last minute.* ☹

Dave's birthday came and went. The day after, it hit me:

rather than try to come up with the perfect reason to convince Willie to meet up with us, perhaps we should approach it from the opposite direction.

I sent a group text suggesting a group reunion *for absolutely no reason!* in Las Vegas.

I'M IN!!!!!! texted Willie within thirty seconds. *WHEN????*

This weekend, I wrote.

IN!!!!!!!! WHAT ARE THE DEETS????

At 8:00 p.m. that Friday night, Josh, Dave, and I met in the Las Vegas suite that we had reserved for the intervention itself—Party Central, as I had called it on the Evite—and started arranging the furniture in what would look like the most casual but serious configuration.

Willie's flight was due in at 9:00.

At 8:30, we got a text from Willie.

Hey—flight delayed for weather. Stuck on the ground for a bit. Sucks. Shouldn't be too long. Will keep you posted.

No worries. How long?

They don't know yet. Will keep you posted, he wrote.

No prob, I wrote. *Excited to see you.*

Whatchu guys doing?!?

I looked around. This was supposed to be a debaucherous weekend in Las Vegas, and it was 8:45 p.m. on a Friday night.

Getting soooo wasted, I texted back.

SOOOO JEALOUS!!!!

Then, twice:

WHO IS THE DRUNKEST??

We looked at one another, and Josh and Dave pointed at me.

Prob me, I wrote back. *Super wasted.*

BWAHAHAHAHAHAHAHA!!!! LOVE IT!!!!!!!!!

We went back to planning when a minor wave of conscience hit me: it probably didn't make a difference, but the text I had just sent was technically glamorizing the drinking we were asking him to give up. It was a subtle thing, but maybe it was the English major in me that thought it would be off-theme to imply that we were having a great time drinking without at least implying some negative consequence.

Feeling sick, I wrote.

BWAHAHAHAHAHAHA U R such an amateur!!!!

This still didn't feel like it had done the job, so I added one more line.

Making some real bad decisions ☹.

What did you do?! BWAHAHAHAHAHAHA tell me!

"What did I do?" I held up the phone.

Dave: "Does he have a macro for 'BWAHAHAHAHA-HAHA'?"

"Probably autocorrect, at this point."

"It needs to be something big," said Josh. "Something he can't just tease you about."

Cheated on Sarah.

Four texts came in from Willie in rapid succession:

W

H

A

fucking T?

Yeah. I know, I wrote back. *Can't believe it. So wasted.*

What happened!?!?!?

Made out with some slut in the bar downstairs, I wrote. "Slut" didn't sound like me, I realized as I read it back. It was a word I used when I was trying to sound like someone else.

Why?? Explain?! he wrote back.

As I held up the phone to show the others, it started ringing in my hand.

"Don't pick up," said Josh. "He'll hear that we aren't really partying."

I sent it to voicemail and texted him:

Reception sucks.

He texted back:

Emailing you—too long to text—hold on . . .

Five minutes later I got an email with no subject:

> Hey! I'm emailing you because this is really important and I hope you really read this and think about it. The first thing you need to do is be honest with *yourself.* Why did this happen, what does it mean, how do you feel about it, and what do you want to happen next. Don't shortchange this or gloss over it. It's not as easy as it sounds. This part will feel hard, and it should—it will actually be harder to be honest with yourself than it will be to be honest with her. Once you are 100% sure you know how *YOU* feel, we can talk about what you do from there. I can't tell you what to do. But as long as you are honest with yourself, we can figure out what is really going on in your heart, and then I will be there to come up with words and actions that are true to that. Anyway. So sorry this is going on. I want you to do the right thing, but first & foremost I want you to know that I am always there for you and always on your side. Stay okay and SEE YOU SOON!!!
>
> —W

I showed it to the room. Everyone read it.

"He could have texted that," said Dave.

An hour later Willie texted the group:

Flight's canceled. SUCKS!!! They put me on the first flight tomor-row & I leave first thing in the morning. Arriving tomorrow noon. Have fun without me. HANG IN THERE GUYS!!!

The next morning we woke up early, arranged the room again, and then got another text from Willie: more delays, in combi-nation with some mileage game he was playing, meant that he was now going to arrive on the same flight as he had originally planned, which would get him in at 8:10 p.m. *Still worth it!!!* he wrote to the group. *Trust me, one night is going to be PLENTY!!!!* Then he sent a separate text to me: *Hanging in there?* I answered that I was.

Now we had to figure out how to spend a whole day in Las Vegas. I texted Sarah—the real Sarah, the best thing in my life, an honorary member of this friend group, close to all of us, a person on whom I had not cheated and never would. Sarah was finishing up her senior year and would then most likely be mov-ing to New York to live with me. She was objectively, by all accounts, in every relevant way, cooler than I was, and would know things like this.

Hmmm . . . Ali Fisher says her sister went to a place for her bach-elorette party called Marquee that was actually kind of amazing in the daytime. Also just fun to hang out in the casinos? How is it? How's the Willie stuff? I started to write back when she started to write more. *Wait—is there something called the Beach Club in your hotel?* I said yes. *Ali Bell's boyfriend Lorenzo says he can get you guys in today and that it's AMAZING.*

I ran it by the group. It turned out that all of us had been secretly intrigued by the excessively but effectively seductive signage for the Beach Club but had assumed it was the kind of place that wouldn't let guys like us in, at least not without a hassle or long wait or being shoved in some miserable general population holding area for an interminable length of time first.

"Sure, if we're really on the list," said Dave.

We really were. And the Beach Club was, as Sarah's friend Ali had promised, amazing. The DJ was great—one of those DJs that surprises you that there have been so many hit songs in your lifetime. There was a lot of bright skin in bright colors, the sun was intense and even, the mixed drinks were the perfect mixture of whatever ingredients had been mixed. I had the actual, literal thought that I was lucky to be alive. I even caught myself wondering whether we'd be on good enough terms with Willie the next day that we could come back here: if we all ordered non-alcoholic drinks, it might still be fun, maybe? The alcohol, it seemed to me, was actually the least important aspect of this experience, maybe? But then again, maybe that was just the alcohol talking?

How are you holding up?

Willie had texted me while I had zoned out. It took me a second to remember what he was referring to.

Okay, I responded. *Thanks so much for caring. I'll be okay.*

Have you decided what to do? How you feel? What you want?

No, trying not to think for now. Just zoning out. It'll be okay.

It will. See you guys in a few hours!!

At around ten past four, it occurred to all of us independently that the afternoon had peaked. "I might want to actually take a nap," said Josh, and we all quickly and enthusiastically agreed. We headed back to the rooms to rest up and made plans to meet back at Party Central at eight and run through the plan once before Willie arrived.

I wasn't used to drinking in the afternoons, and the drinks, probably like all great mixed drinks, turned out to have been much stronger than they felt at the time. I didn't fall asleep until 7:15, and when my phone finally went off at 7:45, I had an unbearable, excruciating headache.

I splashed water on my face and arrived at the room a couple of minutes past eight. I found everyone else in the same state or worse—thudding headaches, eyelids sticking and stinging from leaving their contact lenses in, all from that sun and those drinks that were chased by those awful, worst-idea naps.

"Is there any Advil? Tylenol?"

There wasn't. They had already looked.

Josh turned to me. "Hey. You gotta lead this. I can't do it."

I was in no state to lead this thing.

"You have to lead this," he repeated. "You have to lead this."

I had always heard about the "hair of the dog" cure but had never tried it—officially because it sounded irresponsible, but really because it sounded disgusting. Whenever I was hungover, I thought I never wanted to drink again, let alone right then. But now, with Willie's life potentially at stake, I pulled a beer from the minibar and cracked it open with the hard plastic opener we all had on our key chains.

"What are you doing?"

"Hair of the dog."

"You want Willie to smell alcohol on your breath while—"

"No, I'm going to down it fast, then have some gum."

"You have gum?" said Dave. "Who has gum? I asked if anyone had gum. Who has gum?"

"I'll brush my teeth then."

I swigged the beer and immediately coughed it all up onto the rug, exactly like a baby would if you gave a baby a beer.

"The fuck! Now the place smells like alcohol!"

"We were pretending we partied last night. Remember?!"

"They would have cleaned the room. This is a high-end hotel, you fucking morons!"

Josh reached for two bottles of club soda from the minibar and started spilling them all over the floor on top of the beer with overdiligent evenness.

"That smells worse!!"

"That smells like a gin and tonic!"

"Fuck!!!" said Josh. "This is tonic, not soda!"

"Fuck!!! Where's the soda?"

I couldn't take all this with my headache.

"Where the fuck are you going?"

"Gift shop," I said. "I'm going to get Tylenol. For everyone!"

"Get Advil."

"Get Tylenol."

"Get Advil Extra Strength."

"Get Tylenol Extra Strength!"

"I'll get both."

"Just get the Tylenol! Regular Tylenol!"

"Why the fuck would a person *not* get Extra Strength?!"

"Just hurry back!"

"I will. You make the room look like it's been cleaned."

"Too late for that! That ship has fucking sailed!"

"Our best chance is to make it look like we've been partying all day." Josh started emptying vodka minibottles onto the floor.

"*What* the *fuck*!?" screamed Dave. "Do you realize how expensive that is?!"

"There is a *life* at *stake* here!" screamed Josh.

"How?! Whose?!" screamed Dave.

"Long term!" screamed Josh. "Look! We need a consistent message. And the message is that we got wasted last night!"

"Then what fucking leg do we have to stand on?"

"We'll have to adjust the speeches," said Josh. "Like we all have a problem, but he has the biggest."

"*What?!*"

"Adjust the speeches!"

Dave popped a pill from a prescription bottle.

"The fuck is that?"

"Not Tylenol, don't fucking worry!"

"I'll be right back," I said. "Right back!"

"Wait! What's the opening statement? Who speaks first?"

"What did we decide?"

"We didn't decide."

"Decide!"

I ran out the door to the elevator and headed straight to the lobby, stopping only to accidentally get out of the elevator every time it opened for someone else, which was four times. In the lobby I tried to figure out which direction the gift shop would be in. Everything was a clinking, garish red maze, especially in the state I was in now. The casino looked like a straight person's attempt to replicate what he thought a gay kid he bullied in high school would have designed. I hated Las Vegas. Why hadn't I pushed harder to do this on Dave's birthday? I picked a direction at random and started running as fast as I could, which was not fast at all, in this state. A hand blocked me by the shoulder and knocked me down.

"Where you going, asshole?"

It was Willie. He was dressed in a sharp blue suit, newly pressed, over a crisp white shirt, a garment bag over his shoulder. His shoes were white buckskin, or something along those lines—whatever it was, it looked polished and rare. I was in puffy yellow-and-gray New Balance sneakers that I had promised Sarah I would only wear in the gym but somehow still found myself wearing all the time.

I was embarrassed to be in the same casino as a guy who looked as good as Willie did.

"Hey! Willie!"

He put his hands on my shoulders and took a moment to really take me in.

"You look like shit, my friend."

"I'm okay."

He draped his arm firmly across my shoulders. "Come with me. We need to catch up first. Just you and me."

He walked me up to the bar in the center of the casino and ordered four tequila shots.

I said I was too hungover from earlier in the day.

"Don't make me drink all four of these," he said.

I did what seemed like the less irresponsible action and picked up the tequila shot.

"To health, wealth, and the beauty of our children."

"To health, wealth, and the beauty of our children."

I downed the shot and immediately felt better.

So that's how that worked.

"If you ran for president," said Willie, "and I knew you'd be a terrible president, and you were running against the best president ever—a pro-legalization, pro-gay-rights Reagan—I would vote for you. You know why? Because you support your people. You just do. That's more important than having a good president—having a country where everyone is going to stand by their people, just because they do. Do you know what I mean?"

Two more tequila shots arrived. I dutifully took one and swallowed it. "I'm good for now," said Willie to the bartender.

He turned back to me. "You made a mistake with Sarah. There are no two sides. There is no justification for something like that." I know, I said. "And the fact that we all make mistakes—all of us—doesn't make this one okay." I know, I said. He pushed the other tequila shot in front of me. "Here," he said. That's okay, I'm good, I said.

"No, you really need to drink this," he said. "I need you to drink this before I tell you this."

Willie stared right at me.

I felt sick again. I stared at the drink in front of me.

"Hey. Look at me."

I stared at Willie's forehead.

"I can't let you make a decision without knowing everything. I can't have you thinking everyone's perfect but you. Hey. Look at me."

When I looked him in the eyes, he stared back for a while and either saw something he was looking for or didn't.

"I love you guys. I really do," he finally said. "It's been a really hard first year out. I know it's all going to be worth it, but it's been hard. I know it seems like maybe I have it all together, like I've got it all perfectly figured out, and it's just guys like Dave who are kind of a mess."

We both laughed.

"But yeah, it's hard for me, too. For all of us. The best thing ever is being here with everybody. We really have to do this more often."

"To health, wealth, and the beauty of our children."

"To health, wealth, and the beauty of our children."

He bumped his forehead into mine, hard. When his head hit my head, I noticed that my headache had gone away completely.

"Now where the fuck is everybody?!"

———

As soon as the room key beeped, Josh started shouting from inside the room.

"Did you get Advil or Tylenol?"

I opened the door. The room looked like an absolute mess, the most complicated possible version of pathetic. So did everyone, and everything, except for Willie.

"WHAT'S THE DINKY-DONK, MOTHERFUCKERS?!"

Willie lunged for Dave, torpedoing Dave's stomach with his skull and forcing him onto the bed, coughing. Dave started instinctively defending himself with wrestling moves, which made Willie laugh and break out his own high school wrestling moves.

Josh looked at me, opening his arms, and mouthed, *So?*

I walked to the minibar and opened a beer. Josh stared while I downed the whole thing and threw the empty bottle on the floor.

Then he shrugged.

We got wasted in the room. Then we went to XS at the Wynn, Ghostbar at the Palms, and waited in line at Hakkasan at the MGM until we gave up. Willie won $800 at roulette. Josh hooked up. We got back to the rooms at five a.m., slept till ten, pulled the curtain open, turned up some music, smoked a bowl, and went to the Paris buffet for what we all agreed was the best breakfast, lunch, and dinner of our lives in a single sitting.

"We have to do this more often," said Willie, in a crisp and brilliant benediction over a bottomless bottle of anonymous champagne.

"To health, wealth, and the beauty of our children."
"To health, wealth, and the beauty of our children."
"To health, wealth, and the beauty of our children."
"To health, wealth, and the beauty of our children."

The four of us shared a taxi to the airport together, still drunk from the breakfast. My plane was the last to take off. I played slots until my plane was ready to board. I won, then I lost, then I won, then I lost, all at random. I didn't understand anything, but at least now it was a relief that I wasn't supposed to. Then the plane boarded, and I went back home.

It was the happiest weekend the four of us spent together since college, as well as the last. A few weeks afterward, Willie changed his profile photo to a picture of him surrounded by smiling kids at an inner-city after-school program in a T-shirt with the unexplained acronym H.E.L.P. across it in cursive, and things seemed to get a lot better for him after that. Dave committed suicide six months later.

Wikipedia Brown and the
Case of the Missing Bicycle

It was a quiet Sunday. Wikipedia Brown was sipping lemonade with his friend Sally, when all of a sudden their classmate Joey ran in, out of breath.

"Help!" said Joey. "Someone stole my bike! I left it outside the library this morning. Who stole it?"

"The modern-day chain bicycle was patented in Germany in 1817," said Wikipedia Brown. "Ten-speed bikes became popular in the United States in the 1970s. Carrot Top uses a bicycle as a prop in his popular mainstream comedy act."

"Oooh, Carrot Top," said Joey. "Whatever happened to him?"

"Carrot Top was born Scott Thompson in Big Bear City, California, in 1965," said Wikipedia Brown.

"Big Bear City? What an odd name. Is that a real place?" asked Joey.

"Big Bear City is an unincorporated census-designated location in San Bernardino County, California, with a population of—"

"Wait! Let's not get distracted," said Sally. "Every time we talk to Wikipedia Brown, we get distracted. We spend hours and hours with him, and always forget what we were supposed to investigate in the first place."

"Yes, good point," said Joey. "We have to find my bike. Sally, do you have any ideas?"

"Sally is a bad detective and a well-known slut," said Wikipedia Brown. "Citation needed."

"Is that true?" asked Joey—his intentions unclear.

"No," said Sally, fuming with anger. "I don't know who told him that. It could have been anyone. Literally, *anyone*."

"The government caused 9/11!" Wikipedia Brown shouted suddenly, for no reason.

Sally pulled Wikipedia Brown aside. "Are you sure you're okay, Wikipedia?"

"I'm not perfect," said Wikipedia Brown. "I never said I was. But I work fast, and I work for free, and I'm everyone's best friend. Plus, I'm getting better by the second—and it's all thanks to people like you."

Sally smiled. She liked being part of Wikipedia's process. "Okay, Wikipedia," said Sally. "But I have a question for you, Joey. You say you left your bike outside the library this morning? It's Sunday morning. The library is closed."

Wikipedia Brown stood up with a start.

"George W. Bush is the father of Miley Cyrus's baby!" announced Wikipedia Brown.

This story is under review.

Regret Is Just Perfectionism Plus Time

They all gathered around his hospital bed to cry and watch him die.

"Do you have any regrets, Grandpa?" asked the ten-year-old, solemnly, as if he imagined himself wearing a tie.

"Yes, I do," said the man. "I bought a lottery ticket in 1974. Once. One ticket. Ten million dollar jackpot."

"Did you win?"

"No."

"Were you close?" asked the boy.

"No," moaned the grandfather. "I got all six numbers wrong. All six! I said 12-5-28-4-17-31—that's what I put on the form. If I had put 3-16-18-19-34-1, then everything would have been different."

Chris Hansen at the Justin Bieber Concert

His daughter was dying, literally dying, to go to the Justin Bieber concert, and it was only going to be one night, and her mother was going to be out of town, and it was practically impossible to get tickets anyway except, except! He could always get tickets to anything thanks to his connections as the longtime host of the NBC series *To Catch a Predator.*

But Chris Hansen did not want to go to the Justin Bieber concert.

"I just think," he said, choosing his words to his twelve-year-old daughter carefully, "I just think that my presence there . . . might make some people . . . uncomfortable."

"Who? Pedophiles?" snapped his daughter. "You're afraid of making pedophiles uncomfortable?"

"Yes—no!—I mean . . ." stammered Chris Hansen. "*Look.* Anyone who has followed my career knows I am *not* afraid of making pedophiles uncomfortable. Okay? That's just Chris Hansen 101. Let's get that straight right off the bat."

"Then what *is* it?" she challenged.

Tough girl. His daughter all right.

"What is it, Dad?"

"You want to know what it is?" said Chris Hansen. "You really want to know? I go to the Justin Bieber concert, and everybody's looking at me. You know why? They're looking at me trying to figure out who *I'm* looking at. So everybody's staring at me. And I have to do them the courtesy of not looking back at them, because what they don't realize is that if I look at them back for as much as a split second, then everybody's gonna stare at *them* for the next two hours. You understand why, don't you? And by the way, do you know who's *not* looking at me? There are only a few people at this point who are not looking at me, who are trying to *avoid* eye contact. Do you know who those people are? That's right," said Chris Hansen. "Pedophiles. Those are the pedophiles. So, great, now I know who all the pedophiles are. That's a fun thing to know, isn't it? And now, I am morally obligated to do something—but what do I do? How am I supposed to alert someone in a position of authority that these people are definitely pedophiles who are destroying lives, but that the only evidence I can offer to support this charge is that these alleged pedophiles are suspiciously *not* staring at me? Huh? I'd look like something of an egomaniac, don't you think? So you know what I have to do, to make it tolerable for myself? There's only one thing I can do, Kaitlin. I have to stare straight ahead, *right* at Justin Bieber, never taking my eyes off him, not even for a second. And when people see me at a Justin Bieber concert, staring holes into Justin Bieber, you know what they think? They think, *Ahhh, I see. It all makes sense now.* And I don't even care—I don't have an ego about stuff like that," he lied, "but besides all that, besides *all* that, what about the fact that I bust pedophiles eight hours a day, five days a week, and maybe for once in my life I just want to relax on a Saturday night spending time with my daughter without any of this on my mind?"

She started to cry.

Dammit, thought Chris Hansen. I shouldn't have used that tone. She's just a kid who wanted to go to a concert. I didn't have to make it all about me. Also, I didn't need to exaggerate my hours. It's more like four hours a day, four days a week.

"You know what," he said, "I'll wear a hat or something. It'll be fine."

"You look stupid in hats," she said.

"Hey. That hurt my feelings," he said.

In the end, he took her to the Justin Bieber concert. It wasn't as much fun as she thought it was going to be, and it wasn't as bad as he said it was going to be. The concert was okay, and so were they.

Great Writers Steal

"What if they have an alarm?"

"I told you. We're going to get out too fast for that to matter."

"I don't know. Something feels off."

"Hey! Nothing's off, okay? It's what we're doing. Remember what the book said?"

" 'Good writers borrow, great writers steal.' "

"You want to be a great writer?"

"Yeah."

"Are you sure? Because you don't sound sure."

"I want to be a great writer!"

"You want to be a great writer?"

"Yes! I want to be a great writer! I want to be a legend!"

"Damn right. We're both going to be legends. Kerouac, Burroughs, Bukowski—they probably stole all kinds of stuff."

"Bret Easton Ellis probably still robs places."

"Liquor stores, probably."

"Who knows! Probably. I pictured maybe banks. The point is, we never hear about any of it."

"Right. Right."

"Right?!"

"Right!"

"Ready?!"
"Let's do it!!!"

Neither of them ever got anything published. In fact, those who read their writing went so far as to say that they misunderstood literature on an unusually fundamental level.

But after a few years, they got to be pretty good thieves.

↶ Confucius at Home

"I'm hungry," said Confucius to a nearby servant. "Is there any food around? Some noodles, maybe?"

"CONFUCIUS SAY: BRING NOODLES!" shouted the servant to the cook.

"Hey, hey, please calm down," said Confucius. "It's just a question. Only if it's convenient."

"CONFUCIUS SAY: CALM DOWN!" shouted the servant to the rest of the household.

"Stop it, okay?" snapped Confucius. "Not everything is a *thing*."

"CONFUCIUS SAY: NOT EVERYTHING IS A THING."

Dammit, thought Confucius, and he was about to interrupt him again—but didn't. That one sounded pretty good, he had to admit. And the one before wasn't so bad, either, if interpreted in the right way.

"You get those last two?" Confucius whispered to his scribe, who was sitting in the corner. " 'Calm down,' and the other one?"

The scribe nodded.

"I don't know, maybe." Confucius shrugged. "Not the noodles one, obviously."

But if the scribe wanted to write those other two down . . . well, Confucius wasn't going to stop him.

⌒→ War

The two children began a game of war.

This is a good idea, thought both children. *Soon, I will win. Then the game will be over, I will be happy, and we can both go do other things.*

But no matter how many times they played war, they always forgot how tedious, how tiresome, how emotionally debilitating, how devoid of reward, and how maddeningly left to chance the game was; and how they always regretted having started the contest well before the time it was over.

In that way, it wasn't too unlike the game of bridge.

⌒→ If You Love Something

If you love something, let it go.
If you don't love something, definitely let it go.
Basically, just drop everything, who cares.

⌒→ Just an Idea

When the couple won the $18 millon Powerball jackpot, they found out they had two options. They could accept the state's default payout structure, which would come to $600,000 a year over thirty years; or they could let a company buy the ticket from them for a single upfront payment of ten million dollars.

Both options sounded good.

And they didn't have to decide right away, anyway.

They spent the weekend celebrating in secret with lots of champagne and side dishes.

Rich, forever.

On Monday morning, as they walked up the steps of the Ohio Lottery Commission headquarters, a woman in a business suit intercepted them and presented them with a third option.

An artist named Damien Hirst was in the market for a lottery ticket just like this one, the woman explained. Would they be interested in selling the ticket to him, through her, right now, for the flat fee of twelve million dollars?

"What's he going to do with it?" asked the husband.

"He's going to stamp the word VOID on it and sell it for fifty million dollars."

The wife didn't get that at all, but the husband said he kind of did, maybe.

"We'll talk about it," said the husband. "We'll get back to you tomorrow."

That night they looked up the artist online.

"It's the idea of it," explained the husband. "See? All this stuff. It's the idea."

The next morning they called the woman and told her they'd do it.

"Excellent!" she said.

They signed some paperwork and handed her the ticket, and she handed them a certified check for twelve million dollars.

And even better: nobody had to know they won. They could tell anyone they wanted, or no one if they wanted. No security concerns, no privacy concerns. No sob stories or television cameras or suspicious relatives they'd never heard of.

Just the two of them and the millions and millions of dollars.

The night before they were going to deposit the certified check, the husband awoke so startled by an idea that he had to wake up his wife to run it by her, too.

What if we called the woman back and offered to sell them the twelve-million-dollar check for fifteen million dollars? He could stamp VOID on the check, too!

"I like it," she said.

The next day they called the woman with their proposal that Damien Hirst could buy back their undeposited certified check for fifteen million dollars.

"Why would he do that?" asked the woman.

"Well, he could do whatever he wants with it," said the husband. "For example: he could stamp VOID on the check and then sell that for seventy million dollars."

"Sell what for seventy million dollars?"

"The voided check to us."

The woman sounded perplexed. "I'm sorry, could you explain more . . . what you mean, exactly?"

"You buy the twelve-million-dollar certified check made out to us, George and Cynthia Clark, from Hirst LLC. Okay? You give it to Damien Hirst. He writes VOID or CANCELED on it, or stamps or stencils it or however he wants to do it—he can decide that part."

"Maybe he could paint it in red paint," chimed in Cynthia.

"Shh," said George. "Then you take that, you frame that—he frames that—whoever frames that—doesn't matter—the voided check—that he voided, or an assistant voided, or however he does it—then one of you takes that to a gallery, and you sell it for sixty-five, seventy, a hundred million dollars!"

"I don't think that would sell," the woman finally said.

"Sure it would! It's almost exactly like the first idea, but better!"

"*What* is?"

"The voided check to us! That we gave to him! And he voided! For the lottery ticket that we gave to him! That he voided!"

"I'm sorry," said the woman. "I think I just don't get it."

"That's okay," said the husband.

Just an idea.

Heyyyyy, Rabbits

One morning I looked out my window, and I saw a rabbit hop across my back patio.

Just hopping through.

It entered from one side, then it hopped around a little, then it left out the other side.

That was it.

I loved it.

I wanted it to happen again and again and again.

I thought about buying a rabbit as a pet and putting it on the patio. But I didn't want to have to lock it up in a cage. And I didn't want to let it just roam free, knowing that at any time, anything could happen to it.

I would feel so terrible if something happened to it.

Or if it felt all caged up.

So I put a bowl of carrots out on my back patio.

Heyyyyy, rabbits.

The Best Thing in the World Awards

Many of the nominees were returning: love, Jesus Christ, Julia Louis-Dreyfus on *Seinfeld*, losing gracefully (which never won but was always nominated), sunrises, peace (which was often a finalist during times of war but was otherwise not nominated), summer evenings, the score to *West Side Story*, laughter, Christmas, and peanut-butter-and-jelly sandwiches.

Others were new: internet on planes, spicy tuna on crispy rice.

Beauty had never been nominated. People lived their lives as if it were the best thing in the world, but perhaps in their hearts they knew it wasn't. The same was true for money. Same for honesty.

A lot of people said they thought that Jesus Christ was going to come close one of these days, but it was generally nonreligious people who said that. Believers tended to vote for love, and the more casual believers voted for Christmas, and that split the vote.

Love always won. Everyone knew that and watched anyway. Perhaps even more eagerly, the way that people are more willing to get caught up in a certain type of movie when they have a sense deep down that, of course, love is going to win in the end. The fun isn't whether love is going to win; the fun is in seeing how.

"Welcome to the Best Thing in the World Awards!" announced the host, Neil Patrick Harris. He had been the host for the past four years and he was terrific at it. ("When are *you* going to be nominated?" he was asked each year as he walked the red carpet on the way in, and he'd laugh it off. And so would the viewers at home. "Let's all calm down" was the general reaction whenever anyone would ask Neil Patrick Harris when he was going to be nominated. He was a fundamentally great host, there was no doubt about that; but it said a lot about how seriously people took the awards that he wouldn't be nominated, at least not for a long, long time. An awards-show host? No, sorry. *We love him,* was the unspoken collective answer to this question, *but we're talking about the* best thing in the world *here*.)

"Your votes—you, the viewers at home—are taken into account along with our confidential panel of experts and judges, all to determine the best of the best of the best . . ."

Most people skipped or only half watched the first ninety minutes of the show, which consisted of video segments and live performances celebrating the nominees, all of which had been previously announced. There were dance troupes, some subtitled singing. A man named Louie performed some stand-up comedy, but there wasn't too much he could say on network television. Pixar debuted a ninety-second short film that was, everyone agreed, maybe just average for them but great for anyone else. Oprah Winfrey came out and explained in a smart and accessible way why some of the more-boring-seeming nominees—mostly those involving third world health—were actually really exciting to have on the list.

It was the final half hour that everyone watched intently,

when the three finalists were announced and then narrowed down to two and then, finally, a single winner—the best thing in the world.

The cameras pushed in as Neil Patrick Harris returned to the stage, wearing a crisp blue suit that sharp viewers recognized as the best of its kind.

"The three finalists for the best thing in the world are: Laughter!"

Applause.

"Love!"

Applause.

"And . . . Nothing."

People seemed confused, even Neil Patrick Harris (which everyone knew a host was never supposed to seem—so much for his chances at being nominated next year).

"Uhh . . . Uh, we'll be right back after this commercial break."

When the show returned, Neil Patrick Harris was smiling again. His smile was so reassuring, conveying such a contagious calm, that everyone quickly forgot how he had seemed so unprofessionally off-balance just moments before.

"Ladies and gentlemen, it's time to say good night to one of the three best things in the world. Good night to . . ."

Neil Patrick Harris opened an envelope with the red number 3 on it.

"Laughter!"

Still, amid the laughter, anxiety had settled in among many viewers and especially those in the live studio audience. What did "nothing" mean? Who had nominated it, and how did it make it all the way to the finals on its first time? When love did inevitably win in the end, what would it mean to have "nothing" in second place? Maybe it would enhance the victory for love by placing more distance between love and everything else: "nothing even comes close to love"? Or would it mean that love was only "better than nothing"?

Some of the minds in the room more practiced in anxious thinking were able to wander even farther. If "nothing" were to somehow win—which it wouldn't, but if it did—what would that mean, exactly? Could that still be a victory for love? Would it mean that nothing was better than love? Perhaps it would function as a gentle and welcome reminder that of course, on some level, this entire competition was meaningless—because nothing, no one thing, could really be the best thing in the world? And perhaps that would be profound or even inspiring? Or would it mean something darker than that—perhaps it would mean that all the things that had been thought of as the very best things in the world were still, on some deeper level, less than nothing?

Or maybe this was all a game of semantics: maybe everyone knew what love meant, and everyone knew what nothing meant, and it really was that simple, and that's why everyone was so unsettled?

But it wouldn't even come to that. Love always won, right?

"And now, ladies and gentlemen," said Neil Patrick Harris, laughing elegantly as part of his incomparably seamless transition from laughter's highlight reel to the next award, "now, as we wind down another unforgettable night of miracles big and small, it's time to say goodbye to the second-best thing in the world. Ladies and gentlemen . . ."

Everyone watching, even the people secure in their knowledge that love always won; even those who talked themselves into believing that the infinite vagaries of the word "nothing" meant that its win could mean anything they wanted it to—

everyone—held their breath in the hope that the next thing they saw would be recognizable, somehow, as nothing.

Neil Patrick Harris smiled and began to unpeel the envelope with a red number 2.

"Everyone having a good time? Okay. Ladies and gentlemen, it's time to say good night to the second-best thing in the world. Good night to—"

Screens smashed to pure black, and raw, relieved cheers flew up around the world at the appearance of the highlight reel for nothing—as well as in the television studio, where the lights had short-circuited, and the smart, modern orchestral music subtly omnipresent throughout the broadcast had been replaced with a loud, hollow buzz.

As minute after minute passed, though, collective anxiety started to regroup and return. Why was this taking so long? How long was it going to last? This was already far longer than the other highlight reels, and if it went on much more, the show would be out of time before it was able to play the annually updated highlight reel for love, the much-anticipated traditional ending of the show.

And why, some wondered, had the cut to the highlight reel for nothing been so abrupt? It was a curiously crude transition for a show, and a host, that had never made a misstep like that before.

With less than a minute left in the scheduled program, the lights and broadcast were suddenly back on.

Neil Patrick Harris stood alone onstage. There was no introductory music, no dramatic camera sweep through the crowd. Just a static shot of Neil Patrick Harris and the steady buzz of the microphone soundboard, which had been on the whole time but only now was audible on the broadcast.

Neil Patrick Harris stared straight ahead, pale and determined, looking both intensely focused and intensely disoriented at once, as if a pair of hands had reached inside him, shook him by something as deep and untraceable as integrity itself, and then placed him back exactly where he had stood, the same but forever different.

He also looked, in less abstract terms, as if someone were holding a gun to his head from offstage and forcing him to say something he didn't want to say, which would eventually become a prevailing rumor about the night, backed up over the years, as rumors like this always were, by more and more people with less and less of a connection to the original event.

"The best thing in the world is love," said Neil Patrick Harris. "We're out of time. Good night."

The next year and in all the years that followed, "nothing" was disqualified from competition.

The official statement put forth by the contest organizers explained that the competition was a competition for the best thing in the world, and that nothing was, by definition, "no thing," the absence of a thing, and therefore had "no relevance to the competition."

The logic was sound, even though it did nothing to explain how nothing had come to be nominated that one year; let alone become one of the three finalists; let alone become one of the two finalists; let alone—allegedly, possibly, apparently—come to have its name inside the final winning envelope; let alone who had nominated it, or what in the world it was supposed to have meant.

Whenever anyone asked Neil Patrick Harris about what had

happened on that night, he would simply say, flatly, with a voice he seemed to have long ago deliberately emptied of whatever emotion he might have once had on the subject, "Love won."

Or maybe he was just tired of being asked about it.

Love always won in the end. No matter how it happened, no matter what it took, no matter what it meant. Fair or not, true or not, love won.

If it was a conspiracy, at least it was the best of its kind in the world.

Bingo

"I'm three away across," said Ali, "three away up-down two different ways, and two away diagonal."

"I'm four away up-down four different ways," said Lisa.

"'Four away' isn't a thing," said Brian.

"Yes it is," said Lisa.

"I-29," said the announcer.

"Three away!" reported Lisa.

"That just makes you normal with us," said Brian.

"N-44."

"Three away two different ways!" said Lisa.

"Three away vertical two ways," said Danielle, the oldest cousin. "Three away across one way, two away across one way."

"Two away diagonal one way, three away diagonal another way, two away vertical two ways," said Brian.

"Just two more," said Ali. "Two more, baby."

"G-60."

"One away!" yelled Brian and Ali simultaneously. "One away!" "One away!"

"Two away *three* different ways," said Danielle.

The prize was one hundred dollars, which was a lot if it was 1996 and you were nine, eight, also eight, or eleven and a half years old. This was a hundred dollars that no one even knew existed before Danielle had discovered the sign on the resort's recreation-room door that afternoon and then, in a second miracle, convinced her aunt and uncle that this was the kind of activity that looked like it might be fun for the whole extended family. A hundred dollars, before taxes had been invented and exactly two weeks before the school year was to begin, meant different things to each of them but everything to all of them.

"G-52," said the announcer.

"One away!" said Danielle.

"One away two different ways, two away three different ways, three away a ton of ways," said Ali.

"Two away two different ways," said Lisa.

"One away one way, two away two ways!" said Brian.

"Wait!" said Ali. "The middle space is a free space? I'm one away three different ways!"

"B-35."

"*Bingo,*" said their grandfather from the back.

⌁ Marie's Stupid Boyfriend

No one didn't play the guitar "on principle." Either you can play the guitar, or you can't.

You don't "don't."

Remember him?

⌒→ Pick a Lane

"Pick a lane!!!"

The driver behind me swerved to both sides of my car, leaning his head out the window to scream at me as he honked.

"PICK A LANE!!!"

Here was the thing: both lanes were identical. How was I supposed to decide?

"PICK A LANE!!!!!!"

They were both the exact same width and had the exact same smoothness to the pavement. And there was no one in either lane, either.
Except for me, half in both.

"PICK A LANE!!!!!!!!!!!!!!"

There were little differences, though. The right lane bordered some woods, which were pretty. The left lane was closer to the divider, which made a calming *whoosh* sound as you drove past it.

The thing was, I liked both of these things equally, too.

"PICK A LANE!!!!!!!!!!!!!!!!!!!!!!!!!"

I didn't know which one to pick!

Discussion question:

Which lane should the driver pick?

⌒→ "Everyone Was Singing the Same Song": The Duke of Earl Recalls His Trip to America in June of 1962

The Duke of Earl, raised in privilege and ensconced in luxury, but recently agitated by the achingly beautiful tones of Technicolor in the movies of the palace theater and by a glamorously faded silhouette of the Marlboro Man on the back of a once-glossy magazine that had somehow made its way to the coffee table of the family lake house, decided that it was finally time to see America.

He requested funds for an official state visit, and his request was immediately granted. But he was nervous as he flew in his well-appointed private airplane to the vast and open and young and casual and confident nation. He already knew he liked America, but he didn't know if it would like him.

He went first to the capital, Washington, which was the perfect place to start, as its proud and polished formality spoke a language reassuringly familiar to the duke in him. Then to smart and unruly New York City, and its lovely suburbs in deep and shallow Connecticut; then to Chicago, the tall city in the middle of the wide country; and from there he was taken to a representative handful of farms, big and small, in Illinois, Indiana, and Iowa. He visited a rodeo in the state of Texas, which to his extreme delight was almost exactly as he imagined it; he saw the Grand Canyon of Arizona; and he traveled by train among the optimistic and neatly dressed middle classes to San Francisco, a city so light in every way that he couldn't quite believe his eyes. *This must be what gave them the idea for Technicolor*, he thought, looking out at it; it even made him chuckle out loud now and then, girlishly and by himself, at how pretty it was, yes, but more than anything else how *light*, its hills and its colors and bridges and water and attitudes and people and skies. It made him feel he might somehow float up out of his heavy black shoes into one of the many clouds sitting atop the sunny city, but not just any cloud, a cloud from a children's drawing, puffed and friendly, right next to a sun wearing a movie star's plastic sunglasses and smiling.

And everywhere he went—everywhere—when he introduced himself as the Duke of Earl, the people he met would burst into a wide, friendly grin. He had been nervous, and for fair reason: Americans had no royalty, of course, but beyond that, as every student learned in school, the nation had in fact been born out of a rebellion *against* royalty! And, while anyone in the world might be naturally expected to be at least a little starstruck by, say, the queen of England or the princess of Monaco . . . who, to be honest, had ever heard of the Duke of Earl?

But the Americans, it seemed, to his deep and enduring relief, could not have been more delighted. "Are you really the Duke of Earl, now?" they would ask with that bright, true American smile. One could see the charm lighting up their eyes from some source deep inside them. "Well, isn't that something! The Duke of Earl! I can't wait to tell people I met the real-life Duke of Earl."

And then came the most incredible part: always—inevitably, invariably—within a few moments of being introduced to them as the Duke of Earl, he would catch the Americans humming or gently singing a happy little tune to themselves. But the even more magical part was this: no matter where he was in all of America—the wide streets of Texas, the lawns of Ohio, the pubs of Boston or Philadelphia—*everyone was always singing the same song.*

It was an upbeat song: lovely, happy, sincere, full of joy and life. It was an unmistakably American song. It seemed to be mostly gibberish sounds and melodic repetitions, but there were a few phrases he could make out when people got carried away. *"Yes, I . . ." "Oh I'm gonna love you . . ." "Oh oh . . ." "Nothing can stop me now . . ." "'Cause I'm . . ."*

"What's that song?" he would ask, and the Americans would always immediately snap out of it. "Oh, I didn't realize . . ." they would say, very often blushing. They had never even noticed they had been singing. "Just this silly song, I guess."

"Well, I like it," the Duke of Earl would say. "I like that silly song."

After three weeks, the Duke of Earl returned home. He never went back to America, but he never stopped thinking about it, never stopped talking about it. He had a responsibility, of course, to love and serve the people of Earl above all else, and that he would do—that of course he would do. But in his heart at night, always baffling and delighting him, was America, the vast and varied land where everyone was singing the same song.

⌐∼ The Pleasure of Being Right

"I'll never get over it."

You will, everyone told him.

"I'll never be happy again. It's over, it's all over!"

Of course you will be, they said. Happier, even! You just can't see it now.

But they were wrong, and he was right. He was miserable for forty years, and then he found out it was time to die.

What had they known, after all? They were just saying all that. They didn't have any information that he didn't.

In fact, they'd had considerably less information than he had. They just knew what they thought they were supposed to say, so they said it.

In his final half hour, as he lay in his hospital bed, alone except for a dreadlocked attendant in blue who spoke a different language, now at the end of a life that was indeed defined by despair and meaninglessness—just as he had insisted it would be—his spirits first sank and then lifted as he felt himself slip into a deep and private joy, recognized by all who feel it but known only by a few: the pleasure of being right in the end.

⌒⟶ Strange News

Man Returns to Bank He Robbed for Smaller Bills

BISMARCK, ND—A North Dakota man who had robbed a local bank was arrested after he returned to the same bank window two days later and attempted to exchange his hundred-dollar bills for smaller denominations. "If he wanted twenties, he should have just asked for them the first time," said bank manager William Long, who recognized the suspect's voice from the robbery. "Or just stuck with what he had—I'd say a bag of hundreds can get you pretty far in today's economy!"

Indeed, the world's economy is based entirely upon the collectively held assumption that numbered pieces of paper issued by governments correspond to specific, tangible, and transferable real-world values. These presumed values fluctuate every second in relation to the perceived value of numbered pieces of paper printed in other countries, and also to pieces of metal (see Regular News).

Moose Interrupts Town Meeting on Wildlife Protection

WECK, ID—A town council meeting on whether to vote to extend wildlife protection in a local park got a surprise visitor on Friday: a moose!

Officials say the animal, an adult bull moose, wandered in through an open loading-dock door and interrupted council business for nearly an hour as animal-control workers untangled the antlers from a string of seasonal holiday lights. "I'm a devoted hunter, and I can say I've never seen antlers that big," said Councilman Thomas Ross. "Those were some major antlers."

Scientists have determined that antlers are a result of an imperceptibly incremental evolutionary adaptation over the course of millions of years, a process that began with one single-celled carbon-based life form which traces its own origin to an infinitely small dot of arguably infinite energy that exploded 13.7 billion years ago due to reasons that are thought to be best understood by a man in a wheelchair who speaks through a computerized voice box (see Regular News).

World's Largest Tomato to Become Tomato Sauce

NAPOLI, ITALY—A tomato declared by *Guinness World Records* to be the world's largest tomato will now become tomato sauce, says the farmer who grew it. "We already have the record, now let us celebrate!" said Elio Bianchi III, 52. "What is the point of watching it rot, with so many hungry people out there smacking their lips for delicious pasta?"

Indeed, worldwide totals of food production and of

people living in poverty simultaneously hit all-time highs this year (see Regular News).

Man Sues Brother over Glass of Flat Beer

WIKOSHA, WI—A man took his brother to small claims court to demand compensation for the "annoyance and emotional distress" caused when Saver's Pub, the bar owned by his brother, allegedly served him a glass of flat beer. The man is suing for $160, claiming that the experience "ruined [his] whole night" and that his brother's offer of unlimited Coca-Cola in its stead was "designed to humiliate" the man and "to show everyone that I'm still just his little brother, still drinking Coca-Cola even though I'm a grown adult at a bar."

Coca-Cola, a beverage that was originally designed for the purposes of recreational cocaine use and subsequently adapted as a concoction of uniquely flavored and sweetened carbonated water devoid of nutritional content, spent the past year as the world's most popular and profitable product brand (see Regular News).

Man Finds Coat Button After Twenty-Two Years

KASHMIR—A soldier in the disputed region of Kashmir found a missing button to a coat he was wearing—after twenty-two years!

The button had been lost while his late father, a soldier in the same conflict, took refuge one night in a cave on the battlefield. The son, sleeping in the same cave, and wearing the same coat twenty-two years later, came across the button as he brewed tea.

"It fit perfectly," said the soldier, Kanhaiya Makhan, 23. "The coat looks much better now."

Endless war over minor ideological differences remains one of the most defining aspects of human life well into the 21st century (see Regular News).

Man Receives Text Message from Deceased Relative

INDIANAPOLIS, IN—A 36-year-old man received a text message from his mother reminding him to "stay warm this weekend"—six hours after he had paid his respects at her funeral.

The cell phone provider apologized, citing a rolling power outage at a cellular broadcast tower that led to delayed delivery of some messages for up to three days.

The company offered the customer its apologies as well as a free phone with a year's worth of unlimited data, but the man says he may not take them up on it. "I kind of feel like the message was from her, in a way," said Alex Rossini, 36. "Plus, it's just a phone and a data plan. I think I'm set in that department."

Indeed, most human beings in the developed world already carry a device that can instantaneously access essentially all of the recorded information in history, and the average price of such devices recently hit an all-time low (see Regular News). Nobody knows what happens after death (see Opinions).

⌒→ Never Fall in Love

The day she started as a secret agent, her boss told her one very important rule.

"Never fall in love."

But she did fall in love, almost immediately. Within a month, she was hopelessly and endlessly in love with another secret agent, a kind, warm man named Bob. He had big hands and a lot of brothers and sisters, and there was no falling out of love with Bob.

She went to her boss's office and handed him a letter of resignation.

"Why?" he asked.

"I met someone," she said. "I've fallen in love."

"Who?" he asked.

"Bob."

"I love Bob!" he said, lighting up. "Oh, what a great guy. That's a perfect match, you and Bob! I'm so happy for you."

He then remembered the issue at hand.

"But why are you resigning?"

"I broke the one and only rule you told me," she said. " 'Never fall in love.' I fell in love."

"Oh, honey," he laughed. "That's not a real rule! I just knew you'd never find love if you were looking for it."

⌒ The World's Biggest Rip-Off

Here's a story with a happy ending.

I am a thirty-eight-year-old married father of two. A couple of summers ago, I took our family on our first-ever family vacation.

The plan was to drive from our home in New Hampshire to my wife's parents' lake house in Canada. On the way there, we would stop for a night at the Baseball Hall of Fame. Then a week at the lake house. Then on the drive back we would spend a couple of days at Niagara Falls.

The Baseball Hall of Fame was a disaster. My son hated it, and we had stopped there only for him. Basically, he spent the whole time asking if his favorite players would ever end up in the Hall of Fame, and I told him the truth, which was no, because of steroids. Maybe I should have lied.

The lake house was a disaster, too. My kids somehow got it in their heads that they wanted to watch the movie *The Hangover*. Of course I wasn't going to let them watch *The Hangover*—they were eight and ten years old—but they decided to make the whole week a fight about whether or not they could watch it. My wife's parents thought this whole thing was my fault, because they didn't know what *The Hangover* was and they didn't understand why I wouldn't let two young children watch it.

Niagara Falls was a disaster. My eight-year-old daughter was the one who had begged to see it because a couple from a television show she watched got married there. But when I pointed it out to her from the car window on the drive to our hotel—"Look, Niagara Falls!"—she said it looked different than she thought it would and went back to her book. Great, I thought. We have two days here, and that's all there is to do, and she's the only one who wanted to see it, and she's already bored by it. And that *was* all we did. And it *was* boring.

As we started the drive back home, we passed a sign on the highway for the Guinness World Records Museum, and my kids said they wanted to go. It was the first thing they had wanted the whole trip that I could conceivably let them have, so even though we were already over our budget for the trip, I said okay, let's check it out, and pulled off the highway.

But the museum was a disaster, too. The lines were long, and nothing impressed my kids. Not the World's Largest Watermelon, not the World's Hairiest Woman, not the World's Fastest Toilet. Not the fingernails guy. Nothing.

I was about to call it a day when I saw a small hand-drawn sign above a curtain in a corner:

WORLD'S BIGGEST RIP-OFF. $100 PER PERSON.

I waved my wife over.

"No, no. Absolutely not." She said tickets to the museum had already taken us way over budget for the trip, and we weren't paying a hundred dollars a person for something else now, especially something that the sign said right there was a ripoff. "No, no, no. No way."

Something about it really intrigued me, though. I asked the guy in front of the door, who wasn't wearing official museum gear—just black pants and a black T-shirt—if there was at least a children's rate.

"One hundred dollars a person. No discounts. No refunds. Cash only."

This only made me more intrigued. What the hell was in there? I had to know. But the more interested I got, the more skeptical my wife became. "You know what?" she said. "Fine. Just go in yourself and take a look if you need to know what's in there so bad. We'll wait." But this was a family vacation, I said. Whatever I was about to experience, I wanted to experience with my family.

I told my wife to wait with the kids and I ran out to an ATM down the block. It only let me withdraw up to a $200 limit, so then I ran back and begged my wife to let me borrow her card and tell me her PIN so I could withdraw two hundred dollars more.

At this point, my wife was understandably starting to lose her cool a bit. She said I was acting like a fool and a sucker and some other harsher things that I'd rather not make the effort to remember right now. I'm not going to lie: it was a tense moment in our marriage. Finally, she told me that I was no longer the type of person she could trust with her ATM password, but that if it was this important to me, I could wait in the museum with the kids while she went across the street herself to withdraw two hundred dollars from her card, but that she needed me to know she would "never, ever forget what happened today." I said yes, thank you, it was indeed this important to me.

Fortunately, as I said, this story has a happy ending. Inside the secret room was a mind-blowingly elaborate, incredibly well-executed interactive holographic exhibit on the Bernie Madoff hedge fund scam of 2009. It was beyond amazing—just jaw-droppingly intricate and detailed and smart and interesting and well designed. The holograms actually interacted with you, putting you in the mindset of the people who got ripped off, and very compellingly conveyed the scope of the scam he pulled—did you know the numbers involved? Staggering.

Anyway, all of us were absolutely fascinated. And it kicked off a whole bunch of questions, too. I mean, really, how often do kids ask you questions about how stocks work, how bonds work, what's a manageable risk for an investment, what our investment values are—stuff like that? And it was actually really good for me and my wife, too, to get on the same page. (Especially after what we had gone through that day.)

So anyway: they learned, we learned, we connected, we had fun, and it was a unique experience that we all got to share together and that stayed with all of us. To this day, two years later, I still catch the kids looking over my shoulder while I check the financial news online. And whenever we talk about the trip, which is often, everyone always smiles, and someone inevitably does an imitation of the funny hologram of Bernie that greeted us on the way in, making a really funny, evil-smirky face. "Inveeessst with meeeeee!"

You thought my wife was going to be right on this one, didn't you? Everybody always does when I start to tell them this story. That's okay. She's usually the one who's right about this kind of thing. About everything, actually—I married well. But this time, luckily, I was the one who was right.

⌒➤ The Walk to School on the Day After Labor Day

I was sad that summer was over.
But I was happy that it was over for my enemies, too.

⌐→ Kate Moss

When I was sixteen, I would come home from school every day and stare at pictures of Kate Moss for hours.

Then one day, on a school trip to New York, I saw Kate Moss. I went up to her and pulled her coat.

"Are you Kate Moss?" I said.

"Of course," she said.

"How did you become Kate Moss?"

She moved her face close to mine and smiled and whispered.

"Every day," she said, "when I came home from school, I would stare at pictures of Kate Moss for hours, until one day, I was Kate Moss."

"How many hours?"

"Four."

When I went back home, I tried staring at photos of Kate Moss for four hours a day.

Now I'm Kate Moss.

⌒➔ Welcome to Camp Fantastic for Gifted Teens

Dear Gifted Teen:

Picture, if you will, the heartbreakingly temporary canvas of a summer night. Each moment evaporates into the mist of memory as fast as it can be felt. The muggy scent of summer's stillness is pierced only by the trivial phosphorescence of a mindless firefly. Dead stars linger on in the sky as a sick joke—absence itself masquerading as a panoply of permanence.

This is a typical summer evening for a gifted teen. The pleasures of youth are smothered in the mind's crib by the much-praised pillow of your own awareness. Activities are to be mastered, friends are to be impressed, and life is to be learned, not lived.

Rest assured: there is an escape from what makes you special—and it begins right here.

Camp Fantastic is a place for teens to have sex, do drugs, and stay out of trouble.

Things you can do at Camp Fantastic include . . .

> Read
> Sex
> Play games that you make up
> Drink / Do drugs
> Sleep in bunk beds

Go Fish
Go Fish (card game)
Comic books
War (card game only)
Conversation
Unstructured Free Time
Horseshoes (coming in 2016)
Friendships
Unforgettable memories

At this point, you may be a bit curious about the person writing you this letter. I am a former gifted teen myself. Years of neglect from loved ones about the peculiar challenges of my predicament—particularly with regard to maintaining the delicate and necessary self-restorative cycle of mindfulness and mindlessness that comes much more naturally to those whose inner cerebral acrobatics are not permanently set to emergency-high levels of attention-demand—led to a series of emotional breakdowns over the course of my life that have spangled my generally extraordinary intellect with the welcome-textured scars of impulsive thinking and counterproductive endeavors, as well as flash-bouts of radically unfiltered and unnecessary honesty, some of them on display in this very letter.

After many long and unprofitable years acquiring bottle cap collections and selling them for scrap metal (long story—it's not quite as stupid as it sounds, but essentially the sentimental and historical interest affixed to the bottle caps forced me to buy them at a considerable premium over the value of the metal itself), I found myself facing a brutal foreclosure on my house in the Hamptons. In the ensuing panic, I founded Camp Fantastic, primarily as a tax dodge but also as a way of changing lives for the better.

Today, I am a former millionaire living in an air-conditioned apartment not far from the historic town of Patchogue, New York. Would I give it all up to change places with you, a gifted teen on the cusp of an unforgettable summer of priceless, idle pleasures? Of course not. Being a gifted teen is a walking, waking nightmare. But perhaps, with some time and effort, you can change places with me.

Remember, there is no adult supervision at Camp Fantastic, so be sure to keep an eye out for your own safety and best interests.

As a favor to me, please do not kill yourself at Camp Fantastic. Have a fantastic time.

Pugel Karnopovich, Jr.
Founder, Camp Fantastic

There Is a Fine Line Between Why and Why Not

"There is a very fine line between why and why not," said our graduation speaker.

And the secret of life was to live right on that line.

Or on the "why not?" side.

Or on the "why?" side, but you're always looking over at "why not?" and wondering.

Something like that. None of us remembered. All of these made a lot of sense. Whatever it was, it was a great speech, and if we ever need to know it exactly, we can look it up.

⌐→ The Man Who Told Us About Inflatable Women

"Why do I prefer inflatable women?" asked the old man with a torn-throat chuckle, as if surprised, yet in a way not surprised, to have posed himself this question. "Why do I prefer inflatable women?" he asked again, this time with a shake of his head, as though he just couldn't help being charmed by himself, despite his better wisdom, despite knowing himself all too well.

It was a question on none of our minds. We shot each other little "get me out of here" glances. We didn't want to know. But now, at this point we also didn't want to *not* know, because then we'd always be thinking about it: working it into our group emails as that inside-joke reference you all just had to refer to, eventually out of tradition, long after it had stopped being charming; waking up in the middle of the night with that sudden, quarter-conscious certainty that we had solved it!—but then forgetting the theory by morning; eventually, if it came to this, paying to see one of those "Joke Man" acts that come through the local comedy club from time to time, where the audience is invited to shout out the first parts of jokes so that the Joke Man can prove he knows all the jokes there are to know, and shouting out "Why did the old man prefer inflatable women?" and taking the risk that the Joke Man might actually have the integrity to simply stand there alone in the silence and admit "I never heard that one. What's the punch line?" and you'd have to say, in front of the whole comedy club, that you didn't know either, that it was just a real thing that had genuinely been on your mind.

No, it could only get worse if we didn't find out now.

But it turned out that we didn't have to ask.

"I don't prefer them because they're inflatable," continued the old man, now all of a sudden more than able to answer the question that had seemed to baffle him only seconds earlier.

His old eyes smiled and his old mouth crackled with decaying mischief as he savored one last second of mystery. "I prefer them because they're *deflatable.*"

Oh, gross.

He laughed and rotated his cigar slowly, as though examining it to make sure it was burning evenly, but which he couldn't have been doing, because when he finished rotating it he nodded at it firmly, sure and pleased, even though the cigar wasn't burning even close to evenly by any measure. Then he slid another sip of whiskey down his mouth, and then he laughed some more, softer and softer, until he was laughing in perfect silence, as if a skilled DJ were slowly turning his volume knob down to zero.

It was a tasteless thing to say, but I had to admit he said it in a cool way.

Also, who invited this guy? This was supposed to be a party celebrating Mike's two-year-old's birthday, and I thought he said he was going to keep things small. Mike said he didn't know him.

⌒⟶ A New Hitler

We need a new Hitler.

Let me explain: a new Hitler *nothing* like the old Hitler.

I think we can all agree that the old Hitler was a monster, a maniac, and an evil man.

I'm talking about a *new* Hitler.

I'm talking about a Hitler who's *against* genocide. I'm talking about a Hitler who's *opposed* to world domination. Now, that's the kind of Hitler I might be able to get behind! A Hitler who wants to improve our schools. A Hitler who understands that ordinary Americans need more access to health care—and isn't afraid to tell that to Congress! A *new* Hitler! A *good* Hitler.

Hopefully, the new Hitler would not have the name "Hitler," because I think people might find that distracting.

Constructive Criticism

When it was almost complete, Don took his ten-year-old son to see the office building he had been supervising for almost two years.

Don Junior wanted to be an architect. Just like his dad. That's what he had declared one night over spaghetti and ketchup, and every birthday and Christmas since then—five, in total—had been devoted to toys, then posters, then books about architecture and construction.

"Here. You're gonna have to put this on," said Don, picking up a pair of hard hats from a steel table. "That's the rule."

Yellow hard hats. Standard issue. Just like in the books, in the posters, on the Fisher-Price men.

"Okay, now pull the strap . . . Click it into place. There you go. All set."

It was a special moment, all the more so for how simple it was: handing his son a hard hat on his first visit to a real construction site. But Don couldn't let on how much this moment meant to him, because that would mean letting go of that straight face, and he knew that straight face was a big part of the moment.

———

Don walked his son through the site, pointing out different things he had built and the different decisions that had led to them.

Don Junior took it all in without offering a word or expression.

Don showed him more and talked a little quicker, and Don Junior took that in, too, with the same focused look.

The straight-faced thing apparently came a little easier to his son than to him.

"Well, what do you think?" Don finally asked.

"Can I give you some con-struct-ive criti-cism?" said Don Junior, pronouncing the term carefully.

"Of course!" said Don, smiling and then erasing the smile once he felt his straight face crinkling. "Of course. What do you think?"

"I think the drop-ceiling isn't necessary," said Don Junior. "It kinda just looks like extra empty space."

"That is a very smart observation, Donny! Now, there's an important reason why we used the drop ceiling."

"Oh, I know why you did it," said Don Junior. "It's because you figured you'd run your HVAC through the soffits."

"Exactly right!" said Don.

"But take a look at the width of the elevator shaft," said Don Junior. "That's at least a foot wider than you need for handicap accessibility. You could have run your HVAC up along the sides of the shaft. See?"

"That's good thinking again, Donny. The reason we made it wider is because some tenants have equipment they're going to want to move up and down."

"Then why do you also have a service elevator?"

"That's a good question," acknowledged Don.

"Add up that extra height on each floor, you could have added a ninth or even a tenth story. Too late to do anything about it now."

Don Junior rapped his knuckles on a wall. "Now, what's the function of this wall here?"

"That actually isn't a load-bearing wall," Don explained.

"Yeah, no kidding," said Don Junior. "If you had made it load-bearing, then you could have knocked down this beam in the middle of the room. Or you could have put shear walls on either side of the room, kept the post, and knocked *this* thing down. In either scenario that's an extra fifty square feet of potential space lost on each floor. Too late to do anything about that."

Don Junior pointed to the main entrance. "Nonfritted single-pane glass for the main atrium."

"Yes. Double pane would have been unnecessarily expensive for this climate," said Don.

"Double-pane or fritted single-pane glass would have qualified you for LEED certification and that would have more than made up the difference with tax incentives. Too late to do anything about that now."

Don looked down, and Don Junior followed his father's eyes. "This," Don Junior said, kicking his foot. "This concrete isn't a 3500 mix, is it?"

"2500," said Don.

"For an *eight-story building*?"

Don said nothing.

"Okay, I know I don't have to tell you this, but you're going to start seeing problems in the foundation after about ten, fifteen years. It's beyond me why you wouldn't have gone with 3500 mix for the same cost. This is going to end up being a very expensive mistake. It's a foundation issue, though, so it's too late to do anything about that."

Don tried not to look at anything.

"Crew seems nice," Don Junior offered. "Energized, good communication."

"They're the best," said Don, once again turning to face his son. "Gilbert's guys. I use them for everything."

"Are they union?"

"Yes," said Don.

"Look me in the eye," said Don Junior. "Are they a union crew?"

"No."

"Well, too late to do—"

"Let's go home," said Don.

As they began the walk to the car, Don turned abruptly toward his son.

"Hey. I thought that you said 'constructive criticism.'"

"Yeah!" said Don Junior. "I was criticizing your construction."

"That's, no. That's . . . I guess, that would be 'construction criticism.'"

"What's 'con-struct-ive criti-cism'?" asked Don Junior.

"'Constructive criticism' is when you give criticism when the person still has time to make it better. It's meant to be helpful, not hurtful."

"Ohhhhhhhhh," said Don Junior, sounding like a ten-year-old again. "We just learned about it in school. I must have gotten it mixed up."

"That's okay," said his father. "There's a lot you don't know yet. You're just ten years old. A lot . . ." His father sounded unsure. "A lot . . . Let's go."

Don put the two hard hats back on the table, and then put his hand on his son's shoulder to steady his hurt as they walked to the car.

As they walked, Don Junior tried his best to keep a straight face.

The Bravest Thing I Ever Did

I went to the Transgender Alliance Support Group meeting.

I waited over an hour to speak.

Hearing all the stories.

Finally it was my turn.

"Sometimes, I feel like a man trapped in a woman's body," I said.

Everybody nodded.

"That's how tight my girlfriend's pussy is."

I smirked, holding the smirk just long enough for them all to get it. It took a while, since this was not what they were expecting at all. But I was also careful not to wait so long that I couldn't get the cool comic timing exactly right for my exit.

"Smell ya later," I said with a wink, and walked right out of the room.

It's not always enough to be brave, I realized years later. You have to be brave and contribute something positive, too. Brave on its own is just a party trick.

⌇→ Rome

The couple retired to a villa in Rieti, Italy, that they had learned about from an in-flight magazine feature on affordable retirement destinations. It was about fifty minutes outside of Rome by car, and the husband often went into Rome for errands.

"This car charger isn't working for some reason. I'm going to head into Rome and get a new one."

"Don't they have them in the gas station in town? I'm sure I've seen them there."

"Maybe, but better selection in Rome, probably. Better prices in Rome, too. They're always going to charge you more at a gas station in a small town. It's a convenience fee that you're paying in those places. It's fine, I was going to be heading that way anyway—I've been meaning to swing by Rome to get some garden shears, too. Anything else? I can call you and check when I get to Rome."

He loved saying "Rome" like that. "Head into Rome," "swing by Rome." It was just the nearest place to them. How cool was that! Rome, the city of legends, of conquerors, of history, of myth—this was where he bought *batteries*! The place that people saved up to visit their whole lives: for him, this really was simply the place where he might fill up on gas one day and where the next day he'd have to know the right shop to pick up flowers for his wife to thank her for making dinner—with ingredients he had also picked up in Rome. Rome! That's all Rome was to him! Nothing special at all!

"I should be home by five, or six at the latest. It's Tuesday, so you never know about that rush hour traffic, coming out of Rome."

"Okay. That's fine. See you then."

"See you then!"

And he headed into Rome.

↝ The Literalist's Love Poem

Roses are rose.
Violets are violet.
I love you.

J. C. Audetat, Translator of *Don Quixote*

It wasn't a good time to be a poet, which is what he was. But it was a good time to almost be a poet, which is what he almost was.

"Have you heard this song? It's like poetry."
"I will have to check it out!"

"Have you read this book? It is poetry."
"Oh, no thank you."

J. C. Audetat was born with the talent of a poet, the temperament of a poet, and the particular good looks that are not necessary but happen to be ideal in a poet.

But while poetry was what he was best at, there seemed to be no good place for poetry in his day, except for obscure journals edited by people who didn't particularly impress him and read by people who didn't impress him, either, probably because they were the same people.

This was the minor tragedy of being born with the skills and ambition of J. C. Audetat, who dreamed of being a great poet, and—in a separate but connected dream—of living the life of a great poet. Unlike the precontent pretenders whom the world seemed to consider his contemporaries, J. C. Audetat cared too much about the world to hide away his life's work in such a lonely corner of it. He wanted his words to be everywhere. He wanted them in airports, and he wanted them stolen by teenagers, and he wanted them in bookstores that also sold things.

As he continued to write poetry of high skill but irrelevant impact, J. C. Audetat did his best to claim the rewards that would be due a great poet in an adjacent era through adjacent means.

For the moderate riches due a great poet, he took work within an elite and well-paid circle of freelance magazine writers.

For the adoration due a great poet, he made a point of writing his articles longhand on legal pads in fashionable cafes, always looking like a brilliant, beautiful mess, a priceless piece of set decoration for any independently owned coffee shop: the poet completely lost in his work, pausing only to explain—often, and at length, depending on the questioner—what it was he was working on.

This had been going on, anonymously and happily enough, for several years, when a fan of his at a small division of a big publishing house, impressed by his work but in this case just as intrigued by his name, asked if he might be capable of translation. Without thinking too much about it, Juan Carlos Audetat said sure.

Two and a half years later, J. C. Audetat returned to his commissioner an outstanding draft of what was regarded by many to be the first and finest novel ever written, *Don Quixote*, but in a new translation that brought the "easy humor,"[1] "heart-stopping clarity,"[2] "proto-Falstaffian mischief,"[3] "class,"[4] "intended—but never calculated—immediacy,"[5] "O.G. Euro-Hispano *flava*,"[6] and "rhythms of speech and thought that we recognize less from literature than from life itself"[7] to readers for "the first time in one or—gasp, could it be possible?!—perhaps even many generations."[8]

> "For I would have you know, Sancho, if you do not know it already, that there are just two qualities that inspire love more than any others, and these are great beauty and good repute, and these two qualities are to be found in abundance in Dulcinea, because no woman can equal her in beauty, and few can approach her in good repute. And to put it in a nutshell, I imagine that everything I say is precisely as I say it is, and I depict her in my imagination as I wish her to be ."
>
> — *DON QUIXOTE,* PART I, CHAPTER XXV,
> MIGUEL DE CERVANTES,
> TRANS. JOHN RUTHERFORD

> "For I would have you know, Sancho—if you do not know it already—that there are two qualities that inspire love above all: great beauty and a good name. And as it so happens, both beauty

---

1. Nick Hornby, *The Believer.*
2. Janet Maslin, *New York Times.*
3. Harold Bloom, *Yale Book Review.*
4. Brian Lewis, *Men's Health.*
5. Keith Gessen, *N+1.*
6. Junot Díaz, *New York Times Book Review.*
7. Frank Rich, *New York.*
8. Camille Paglia, *Salon.*

and reputation reach the pinnacle of all possibility in Dulcinea. Few can approach her name, and none can equal her beauty. And I know that everything I say is true, because I see her in my imagination exactly as I wish her to be—and when anything is seen as completely and precisely as I see her, Sancho, then what else can it be called but the truth?"

— *DON QUIXOTE*, PART I, CHAPTER XXV,
MIGUEL DE CERVANTES,
TRANS. J. C. AUDETAT

J. C. Audetat's translation of *Don Quixote* electrified the English-speaking world with the restored size and specificity of the novel's comedy, its love, its hopefulness and foolishness and hopefulness all over again. The words were clear again, the ideas were big again, and the cover was cool. It was for sale at bookstores on college campuses and at clothing stores next to college campuses and sold extraordinarily well in all of them.

The new translation of *Don Quixote* wasn't read by readers, but by everyone. For the first time since Spain at the turn of the seventeenth century, it became not-strange for a friend or a neighbor to snort out loud with an involuntary laugh over an image from *Don Quixote* or for someone to say on a second date, "You know how in *Don Quixote* when . . . ?" out of an attempt to connect, not an attempt to impress.

Some even said the translation was "like poetry."

In the wake of *Don Quixote*'s unexpected and outsize success, J. C. Audetat moved to Paris—or, as he renamed it in his mind, almost-Paris—to live the life of an almost-famous almost-poet.

He found that if he stuck to the right neighborhoods, drank a glass of something hot or cold, and squinted a bit, the Paris in his eyes would look pretty much the way he had always imagined Paris was meant to look. Which was no small thing.

He took a small apartment and spent the days in cafés, idly turning minor thoughts back and forth in his mind and waiting to be interrupted.

In the moments between the interruptions, Audetat wrote poetry. When he finished something, he submitted it to literary magazines and journals, and by and large they published it, and by and large, those who reviewed poetry praised it.

And that was it.

Maybe that was all being a great poet meant, in his time.

Or maybe he simply wasn't a great poet.

Each thought calmed and agitated him in equal measure.

Audetat let the afternoons slip away from his table at the Café de Flore while he passed the time with the rarefied nonwriting he had waited for the chance to do his entire life.

He asked to receive his mail at the cafe—a spectacularly inconvenient option he had chosen purely for show that brilliantly burnished the almost-Paris image of both Audetat and the café. Most of the packages contained dusty hardcovers that seemed to have been FedExed directly from medieval Spain, Post-it'ed in man-made colors with shyly formal suggestions that "perhaps this might spark your brilliant imagination with regards to a *Quixote* follow-up."

The only value of these unopenably dull manuscripts was as a conversation starter.

Hey, what's that?

This?

Then Audetat got his chance to explain who he was and what he had done so far. He sharpened his monologue by the day as he explained again and again why it was so funny that none of these supposedly sophisticated people could understand something that clearly came naturally to his audience right here at the Café de Flore: that *Don Quixote* stood as apart from the rest of its era as the *Mona Lisa* did from its own now irrelevant contemporaries in that long hallway of the Louvre. There was a spark of the current running through each of those works—so to speak, of course, expanded Audetat; the two works, in fact, had far more in common with each other than with their contemporaries.

Let's say the Mona Lisa *is your favorite painting. Okay? So what's your second-favorite painting? Is it another Italian portrait from 1504? See, the hands that were up are coming down. You're laughing, but you get what I mean. Okay, so, similarly . . .*

All the tourists would listen, rapt, inspired, flattered. While they never had read any other literature from medieval Spain, they had often been to the Louvre as recently as that day, and they were always happy to learn that it wasn't their fault that they hadn't remembered anything in the entire museum other than the *Mona Lisa.*

But while Audetat was getting better and better at talking about the biggest question he faced, when the café closed each night, he found he still wasn't any closer to answering it.

How does one follow up *Don Quixote?* Even—especially—if you're just the translator?

He once again ran through and extended the shelf of Spanish-language literature he had been browsing in his mind.

Gabriel García Márquez?

The original translations were still good, relevant, powerful.

Borges?

He loved Borges, but it didn't feel destined for a major translation. It was, perhaps, too cool to catch fire; it seemed expressly written to be discovered in a lightless nook of a library or basement or, best, basement library. Plus, Audetat knew, part of the fun of loving Borges was in being one of the few to love Borges and in passionately recommending him to people who you secretly knew probably wouldn't like him as much as you did.

Neruda?

Pablo Neruda was about as pretty and pure as poetry could get, understandably and deservedly timeless and popular. But anyone who had ever ordered tacos could translate Neruda without much help. Nothing much to do there.

Lorca?

Vargas Llosa?

Eh.

He looked out the café window at the colorful leaves and scarves dotted across the girls of almost-Paris in October and wondered if he would translate anything at all. All that held his true interest right now was this scene in front of him and the desire he had, heightened as it was by living in an age that is supposed to know better, to be a part of it, to disappear into that sentimental idea of the life of the Paris writer that the rational side of him knew had expired long before he had arrived. Sad that he could never live in the Paris he remembered once dreaming of in his youth, he let his mind wander off across life and literature until it settled almost independently on the gnawing notion that perhaps the most true and timeless version of Paris, for everyone, might be a version of this one—the Paris filtered through remembered dreams.

Then he knew what to write next.

"No sooner had the warm liquid mixed with the crumbs that touched my palate than a shudder ran through me and I stopped, intent upon the extraordinary thing that was happening to me. An exquisite pleasure had invaded my senses, something isolated, detached, with no suggestion of its origin. And at once the vicissitudes of life had become indifferent to me, its disasters innocuous, its brevity illusory—this new sensation having had on me the effect which love has of filling me with a precious essence; or rather this essence was not in me, it was me . . . Whence did it come? What did it mean? How could I seize and apprehend it? . . . And suddenly the memory revealed itself. The taste was that of the little piece of madeleine which on Sunday mornings at Combray (because on those mornings I did not go out before mass), when I went to say good morning to her in her bedroom, my aunt Léonie used to give me, dipping it first in her own cup of tea or tisane. The sight of the little madeleine had recalled nothing to my mind before I tasted it. And all from my cup of tea."

— *REMEMBRANCE OF THINGS PAST,*

MARCEL PROUST,

TRANS. C. K. SCOTT MONCRIEFF

"In the instant that this crumble-soaked softness touched my tongue, everything stopped, and the entirety of the world became this feeling that was happening to me. An exquisite pleasure had encircled and then invaded my senses. A feeling isolated, detached, with no hint or suggestion of its origin. And at once, the million misdirections of life had become irrelevant to me, its disasters innocuous to me, its brevity illusory to me—this new sensation having had on me the effect which love has of filling one with a priceless essence. Except that this essence was not in me—it was me . . . Where did it come from? What did it mean? How could I steal it and keep it? . . . Just as suddenly the memory revealed itself. The taste was that of the little piece of madeleine which my aunt Léonie used to give me when I went to say good morning to her in her bedroom, on Sunday mornings at Combray, dipping it first in her own cup of tea. (On those mornings, I didn't go out before mass.) The sight of that little madeleine had brought up nothing to me before I tasted it. And then, all—and all from my cup of tea."

—*THE SEARCH FOR LOST TIME,*

MARCEL PROUST,

TRANS. J. C. AUDETAT

Everyone who had ever said that they wanted to read Proust "someday" found that someday had arrived, as Proust shot from deep in the middle of the alphabetized classics sections to the front shelf of top sellers.

It is an inside joke of history that its most exciting adventures inevitably end their careers as homework. Beheadings, rebellions, thousand-year wars, incest on the royal throne, electricity, art, opera, dogs in outer space. By this, the once-pop writings of Proust—like those of Cervantes before—had been quietly serving out an indefinite sentence in homework bins for generations. But now, Proust's words were back to what they were originally intended to be: once again, kids cheated on their homework so they would have more time to read Proust.

"As a work of literature, simply beautiful . . . As a feat of translation, a thrilling surprise in a field that is, by definition, not prone to many surprises."[9]

"Like the tea-soaked crumbs of its famous madeleine, J. C. Audetat's vibrant new translation of Proust brings the full power of the past surging back towards us at full, thrilling force."[10]

---

9. Dan Chiasson, *Harper's Magazine.*
10. Alan Green, *New York Review of Books.*

"Audetat blows the cookie crumbs off Proust and introduces him—nearly a hundred years after his death—as the voice not only of his era, but of ours."[11]

"In its cracked-out vitality, Audetat's translation blows the reader backward in his chair like he's the guy in that iconic Hitachi Maxell speaker ad from the 1980s, except swap out that subwoofer for a madeleine with an electric current jamming through it."[12]

"As delicious as a madeline [sic] cookie!"[13]

There was no reason, once people thought about it, that an American poet who could translate Spanish, and who lived in Paris, might not be capable of translating a work of French as well. But no one had thought to expect it, and so the surprise revelation that he knew *two* languages well enough to turn their respective masterpieces into modern translations of now-unparalleled quality meant that the work exhilarated not only on its merits but additionally for its audacity. The imagined picture of J. C. Audetat, famed popularizer of *Don Quixote*, casually huddled with his old-fashioned paper and pens in the midst of the beeping and buzzing cafés of modern Paris to bring Proust back into the modern mind, itself became an irresistible image that floated above the new classic like an invisible book jacket and built further, unprecedented anticipation for what was to follow.

---

11. Natasha Vargas-Cooper, *The Awl*.
12. Chuck Klosterman, *New York Times Book Review*.
13. Lauren Leto, *Glamour*.

———

Which was . . . what?

He started writing poetry again, but it didn't come as easily. It was hard now to get past the self-consciousness—the silliness, really—of being such a well-established adult applying himself, seriously, to such a youthful joy.

A poet? Was that something to call oneself? Was that something to be?

He carried his old notebooks of poetry to the Café de Flore to see what he could learn. For hours, the notebooks sat on the table, and Audetat sat in dread. He wasn't sure if he was hoping he would find it good, or bad, or which he feared more.

When he finally opened the notebooks, he found that he liked his old poetry. Loved it, even. It was young, unlike Audetat, and it was unafraid to be seen as foolish, unlike Audetat. But he also knew when he saw the poems that he wasn't a poet anymore.

At least he had been one, once.

Maybe the timing just hadn't been right. Maybe in the past, it would have been something. Maybe in the future, it would be something.

Now it was now, and now what?

Translator's block: Does that exist? wondered Audetat.

Audetat left almost-Paris, reasoning that no one there would care too much about the English translator of Proust, and set out on a university tour of the United States. He spoke about the art of translation to full, grand auditoriums everywhere he went, the ones normally reserved only for visiting dignitaries and the most profane comedians of the day.

People didn't know exactly how many languages Audetat

spoke (his college transcripts revealed Latin, but no other clues) and that mystery had become part of his legend. But the one language that he spoke unquestionably well, in public and in private, was the off-the-cuff vernacular of his day.

"What's next?" was the most anticipated question at Audetat's lectures. It was usually the last question, too, as if the rooms somehow always had the collective intelligence to save their best question for the end.

"I have no idea," Audetat would say. "Any suggestions?" He cupped a hand to his ear, knowing the audience would enjoy getting the last laugh.

"*Anna Karenina!*" "*The Odyssey!*" "Confucius! No—Mao!"

"Some . . . interesting suggestions," Audetat would say dryly, to more laughter. "All present some challenges. Anyway. Thank you so much for coming. See you at the bar."

Afterward, he'd whisper to the student organizers a question he had learned long ago always had exactly one answer per town—"Is there a bar around here where writers hang out?"—and then headed out to Fox Head Tavern in Iowa City or Bukowksi's in Boston (which Audetat thought sounded too on the nose to be authentic and was right) and ordered a drink where people would be most likely to start a shy, respectful conversation with him and where he could disappear into his two favorite pastimes: the poetry of everyday conversations and the people who thought he was brilliant.

After a while, somehow, this got boring, too.

"All happy families are alike; each unhappy family is unhappy in its own way."

—*ANNA KARENINA,*

LEO TOLSTOY,

TRANS. RICHARD PEVEAR AND LARISSA VOLOKHONSKY

"All happy families are alike.

"Every unhappy family is unhappy in its own way."

— *ANNA KARENINA,*

LEO TOLSTOY,

TRANS. J. C. AUDETAT

The new translation of *Anna Karenina* was not a particularly dramatic departure from most major translations that had come before it—and that was part of what made it legendary.

A nearly thousand-page novel, written originally in the plain-spoken Russian of the nineteenth century and translated into English by a poet who had so far only proven his abilities in the relatively related languages of Spanish and French, would understandably tempt the translator to make a "statement" with it, went the unanimous consensus—something at least somewhat equivalent to the extraordinary challenge.

But Audetat's grandest statement was simply the fact of the work itself: the fact that he was somehow able to do this work, and had chosen these works, and that now, on the bestseller lists and bedside tables alike, one could find *Don Quixote* by Cervantes and *The Search for Lost Time* by Proust and *Anna Karenina* by Tolstoy, one stacked on top of the next, all excellent, all relevant, all because of Audetat.

"Just as Tolstoy had a perfect ear for the language of his day, Audetat has a perfect ear for the language of his."[14]

"*Anna Karenina* has once again become the modern story it had always been meant to be."[15]

---

14. Ed Skoff, *The Atlantic.*
15. Lev Grossman, *Time.*

"Admit it: you started Audetat's *Anna Karenina* as a hate-read. You wanted a front-row seat to this overdue literary monster-truck pile-up. Who is this Romance-language proficient American—some friendless kid who opted to take both Spanish *and* French in eighth grade, fine, good for him—to try to delve into eighteenth-century Russian? Admit it: you were excited for *Anna Karenina* to be his *Interiors*, his *1941*, his *Funny People* or (depending on your point of view) *This Is 40*—basically, the one that finally gives you permission to stop waking up in a panic-sweat of misery in the middle of the night to cross-check his Wikipedia bio against your own life and obsess over exactly what they had accomplished by the age you are now. Well, sorry. This motherf***** is as perfect as ever. Come for the hate, but stay for the love. Just don't read the last few chapters on the F train, or you might be tempted to jump off it."[16]

"The question that must necessarily paralyse the world of writers and readers alike, in the wake of the incomparable artistic and commercial success of J. C. Audetat's *Anna Karenina*, is simply: what next? If the past is prologue, we know that one of the greatest books in the history of the world is about to be released and rightfully dominate the planet's conversation. How can any reader—let alone writer—think of any other question in the meantime?"[17]

What other languages did he know? What other interests did he have? What other great books were most worthy, or most ready, or most easily mistaken as such?

---

16. (reviewer anonymous), *Gawker.*
17. Andrew Sullivan, *Times Literary Supplement.*

The speculation over the next book J. C. Audetat would introduce to his age itself became a guessing game with obsessive echoes in the literary world and beyond. Book clubs turned into betting pools. Graphic designers drew up new covers for old classics, just as daydreams. Professors and high-profile fans around the world campaigned exuberantly for their favorite works. A rumored Audetat translation of *The Metamorphoses* briefly crashed servers at the University of California at Berkeley before it was debunked as a hoax. Philip Roth composed an open letter to the *New York Times*, humbly requesting that Audetat consider translating Milan Kundera; Michel Houellebecq, apparently knowing no other tone, published a blistering and inexplicably misogynistic open letter to *Le Monde*, rudely daring Audetat to translate one of his own books, a gambit for attention that went widely ignored. A consortium of undergraduates and professors at Yale University started an online petition for "J. C. Audetat to Translate an Emerging Voice of Color and/ or Gender" that received more than 140,000 distinct units of social media approval online.

The most attention and interest came from a full-page advertisement that ran across many publications and was signed by a notably wide-ranging group that included Bill Clinton, the Aga Khan, Benjamin Netanyahu, Ayatollah Ali Khamenei, Noam Chomsky, Salman Rushdie, Mos Def, Richard Dawkins, former pope Joseph Ratzinger, and over three hundred prominent others who might at first glance seem to have contradictory or at least divergent agendas. "Dear J. C. Audetat," it began—as though there could be a pretext of anything either traditional or intimate about this group sending this message in this way— and then proceeded to lay out the case for Audetat that "a true translation of the *Koran* for the present day could carry a power even beyond the grandness and beauty of the text itself; it might inspire all sides of a fractured world to understand itself better. Consider using the light of your brilliance to brighten the pages of the book that is more discussed while being less understood than any other. We do not intend to place any pressure on the delicate and mysterious force of your talent, but merely to inform you of a way by which the fate of the world may well be moved by the hand that holds your pen."

J. C. Audetat was a different person now. His light had been replaced by a glow. He was forty-four years old and lived far from the center of this activity, in a house near a lake with the loveliest person he had met on his adventures and their two-year-old son. He had chosen both Tennessee and Aurelia in large part for the sounds of their names, and his lifelong trust in the poetic had not led him astray; his life was soaked in brunette tones and accidental music, and he was, for the most part, a happy person.

He took walks most mornings and most evenings on a ragged path that led from his house to the lake and around it and back, letting his mind drift in similarly ragged circles. He walked the path alone, except for a few welcome occasions when he was joined by the one neighbor he knew, a kind and curious man obsessed with the prospect of moon travel whom Audetat came to like and one afternoon helped to compose an unsolicited editorial on the subject for a local newspaper.

Once in a while, Audetat came across something that made him want to write—a flash of ambition, or a filament of beauty that momentarily longed for replication. If he still felt that way when he returned to the house, he would write a note to himself describing in the sparest of terms what the thought had been.

But, luckily or not, the need to write always went away before he felt the need to really do anything about it.

———

One day, it didn't.

One day, on a walk around the lake like every other, Audetat kicked a rock along the path and then, for no reason he could pinpoint other than that this idea had been stalking him patiently for a long time and waiting for precisely the right moment to ambush him, Audetat was jumped by an excitement-coated despair that shouted at him that this daily life—all he could ever have hoped for, as a different, calmer, narrower voice in his head enumerated reasons for every morning—was not a reward but a procrastination; the loveliest and lightest procrastination that anyone could ever have invented for him, but a procrastination nonetheless.

He rushed back inside and set out to find something that would quiet the voice that had just grabbed him and shaken him, almost literally.

He knew he wasn't a poet anymore. Still, while he didn't know exactly what he wanted to say, he knew exactly how it should sound. He knew the acoustics of his age, he knew the precise echo that greatness made within it, and now, as much as he loved—finally—everything in his life, all he wanted was to hear that sound. He needed that sound to pull him out of where he was now, not because he didn't love where he was now, but because he did, so much, that he needed to find out if he could make a sound that could compete with it.

"He must have felt that he had lost the old warm world, paid a high price for living too long with a single dream. He must have looked up at an unfamiliar sky through frightening leaves and shivered as he found what a grotesque thing a rose is and how raw the sunlight was upon the scarcely created grass. A new world, material without being real, where poor ghosts, breathing dreams like air, drifted fortuitously about . . . like that ashen, fantastic figure gliding toward him through the amorphous trees."

— *THE GREAT GATSBY,*

F. SCOTT FITZGERALD

He must have felt that he had lost the world he'd known, that he had finally defaulted on the impossible price of living so long with one dream. He must have looked up at an unfamiliar sky through frightening leaves and shivered as he found what a grotesque thing a rose is, and how raw the sunlight was upon the scarcely created grass. A new world: material without being real, where poor ghosts, breathing dreams like air, drifted about, neither by chance nor design . . . like that ashen, fantastic figure gliding towards him through the once-familiar trees.

— *THE GREAT GATSBY,*

F. SCOTT FITZGERALD,

TRANS. J. C. AUDETAT

The world took a moment to figure out what it was reading. Then another moment.

"At first glance, an English-to-English translation of *The Great Gatsby* would seem to be the very last thing we need. But *The Great Gatsby* has already been translated many times since its publication: into film by Baz Luhrmann, into life by Jay Z. In this context, Audetat's translation is not only the most contemporary, but the most faithful."[18]

---

18. Nathan Rabin, *The A.V. Club.*

"As the definitive fable of American success—the real, the imagined, and the imagined-as-real—*Gatsby* is still inexorably tied to its emblematic author, Francis Scott Fitzgerald, and to its time, the 1920s. This translation of *Gatsby* is the same book, but with its colors refreshed, its lines reinforced, its themes reshaded. But most important, the novel's tumultuous and defining romance with the nature of success is now filtered to us not through the experiences of the great literary star of another era, but through the great literary star of ours."[19]

"The *Gatsby* for our time."[20]

"The timelessness of *The Great Gatsby* is not evidence that we don't need this translation—it is proof that we do. We deserve to read this book as effortlessly as the original readers did, without needing to time-travel back to a place of distancingly different idioms and issues. If you want to read the *Great Gatsby* in 2013, the way that Fitzgerald intended *The Great Gatsby* be read in 1925—read Audetat's translation."[21]

"I loved it!"[22]

"A landmark insult—not only to Fitzgerald and to *Gatsby*, but to literature itself."[23]

"A joke. And not a funny one. F."[24]

---

19. Alan Cheuse, *NPR.*
20. Tina Brown, *The Daily Beast.*
21. Marjorie Garber, *Harvard Book Review.*
22. Larry King, larryking.com.
23. Hector Tobar, *Los Angeles Times.*
24. Jeff Giles, *Entertainment Weekly.*

"The Emperor himself has come before the masses and declared himself naked—and *still*, people praise his robe?"[25]

"Has the world lost its goddamn mind?!"[26]

It was the last thing J. C. Audetat wrote, and the last thing he needed to write. He had now said all he had felt the need to say in his particular life. It was nothing that hadn't been said before, but he had said it all better than it had ever been said in the language of his own time and place.

Which was, in fact, the only language he knew.

Audetat stayed at his home, safely surrounded with the rewards that the original mischief of the compromises of his artistic journey had brought him, as the buzzing of the many minds he had touched vibrated incessantly and harmlessly about him, around him, and through him, like radio waves, for the rest of his life.

It felt like poetry.

---

25. Andrew Sullivan, Andrewsullivan.com.
26. Stephen King, private correspondence with Amy Tan.

↪ Discussion Questions

- Did you think the book was funny? Why or why not?

- Did you flip through the book and read the shortest stories first? The author does that, too.

- What is quantum nonlocality? Be concise.

- Do you think discussion questions can be unfairly leading sometimes? Why?

- Who are we supposed to be discussing these questions with?

- Do you normally have discussions in response to a question that was posed by a person not participating in the discussion? Why or why not?

- Do you think "why not?" is ultimately a better question than "why?"

- Why or why not?

⌒⟶ ACKNOWLEDGMENTS

This book developed alongside a series of public readings in front of live audiences. First and above all I want to thank every person who attended one of these readings. You were the most inspiring of motivators and most honest of editors. I loved you and feared you.

Thanks as well to the staffs of the venues that coordinated these readings: most notably the Upright Citizens Brigade Theater in Los Angeles, as well as its counterpart in New York City; and additionally the Last Bookstore in Los Angeles, Vroman's Bookstore in Pasadena, as well as Shakespeare and Company in Paris.

A few close and trusted friends read this book at various key stages and offered invaluable suggestions and support. I am deeply grateful and indebted to Jeremy Bronson, Lena Dunham, Steve Jeppson, Josh Lambert, Zara Lisbon, Alina Mankin, John Mayer, Mai-Lan Pham, Keri Pina, Rivka Rossi, Alexandra Ruddy, Brittney Segal, Chess Stetson, Jennifer Stetson, Ava Tramer, and Ricky Van Veen.

My literary agent, Richard Abate, took me from person-with-pages to author. His advice and insight along the way have been extraordinary.

My manager, Michael Price, devoted an eye of unmatched dedication and care to this book, from the earliest notions to the final copy edits. He improved every page.

Tim O'Connell and Robin Desser offered exceptional editorial guidance on matters big and small. Paul Bogaards, Gabrielle Brooks, and the entire team at Knopf/Random House all earn my continuing admiration and gratitude for their unparalleled skill and dedication.

Years ago, I shared a lunch with the actor John Stamos. While we did not discuss any aspect of this book, I felt that it would be fun to include his name as a surprise for anyone casually scanning this section for names of celebrities.

My father, William Novak, taught me early and by example that a writer is a perfectly fine thing to be, and that a clear voice is the best kind to aspire to have. His advice on this book was of the highest quality on every level, and the experience of discussing it with him was meaningful on another level altogether. My mother, Linda Novak, provided edits as incisive as anyone's, as well as encouragement so articulate and persuasive that it didn't occur to me until months later that she might be biased. My brothers, Jesse Novak and Lev Novak, offered smart suggestions whenever asked, and treasured support whether I asked or not. Keough Novak was no help at all.

Mindy Kaling gets her own line in the acknowledgments, as previously negotiated by her representatives. Thanks, Mindy. I love you and you're the best.

Josh Funk and Hunter Fraser: we haven't been in touch in years, but you made me feel like the funniest kid in the world. I would stay up late on school nights to write things to try to make you laugh the next day in class, and you inspired the one piece of advice on writing that I've ever felt qualified to give: write for the kid sitting next to you.

A NOTE ABOUT THE AUTHOR

Benjamin (B.J.) Novak is a writer and actor best known for his work on the Emmy Award–winning American television series *The Office*, on which he contributed as an actor, writer, director, and executive producer. He is also known for his standup comedy performances and for his appearances in films such as *Inglourious Basterds* and *Saving Mr. Banks*. This is his first published collection.

A NOTE ON THE TYPE

This book was set in Janson, a typeface long thought to have been made by the Dutchman Anton Janson. These types are actually the work of Nicholas Kis (1650–1702), a Hungarian, and are an excellent example of the influential and sturdy Dutch types that prevailed in England up to the time William Caslon (1692–1766) developed his own incomparable designs from them.

Composed by North Market Street Graphics,
Lancaster, Pennsylvania

Printed and bound by Berryville Graphics,
Berryville, Virginia

Designed by Claudia Martinez